Praise for *The Actual & Truthful Adventures of Becky Thatcher*

★"A delightfully clever debut."
—*Publishers Weekly*, starred review

"The deliciously impetuous, devilishy clever, and uncommonly brave Becky Thatcher is now one of my all-time favorite heroines, and I'm desperate to follow her on more adventures. Captivating, exciting, and great barrels-full of fun, this is a book to adore."
—Anne Ursu, author of *The Real Boy* and *Breadcrumbs*

"Young readers will race through this adventure, while teachers and adults will delight in its gold mine of creative parallels."
—BookPage

"Lawson provides an ingenious tale purporting to reveal Twain's characters for who they really were."
—The Center for Fiction

"[R]eaders not familiar with Twain's work will find an enjoyable adventure story with glimmers of mystery. Fans of historical fiction will enjoy the charming heroine and fitting affirmations of family, friendship, and remembrance."
—*School Library Journal*

"Delightful."
—*Kirkus Reviews*

Mississippi River

Old Cave

Picnic Grounds

Carver Hill

Town Kissing Oak

St. Petersburg Cemetery

11

14

Becky Thatcher's
ST. PETERSBURG, MISSOURI
1860

Main Street

Willow Street

Livery
(Horse Stables)

Sawmill

9. Ruth Bumpner Home
10. Tom and Sid Sawyer Home
11. Mrs. Sprague Home
12. Church

13. Becky Thatcher Home
14. Schoolhouse
15. Amy Lawrence Home
■ Shops. Butcher. Tailor. etc.

ALSO BY JESSICA LAWSON

Nooks & Crannies

The ACTUAL & TRUTHFUL ADVENTURES of BECKY THATCHER

Jessica Lawson

ILLUSTRATED BY IACOPO BRUNO

SIMON & SCHUSTER BOOKS FOR YOUNG READERS

NEW YORK · LONDON · TORONTO · SYDNEY · NEW DELHI

SIMON & SCHUSTER BOOKS FOR YOUNG READERS
An imprint of Simon & Schuster Children's Publishing Division
1230 Avenue of the Americas, New York, New York 10020

This book is a work of fiction. Any references to historical events, real people, or real places are used fictitiously. Other names, characters, places, and events are products of the author's imagination, and any resemblance to actual events or places or persons, living or dead, is entirely coincidental.

Text copyright © 2014 by Jessica Lawson
Illustrations copyright © 2014 by Iacapo Bruno
All rights reserved, including the right of reproduction in whole or in part in any form.
SIMON & SCHUSTER BOOKS FOR YOUNG READERS is a trademark of Simon & Schuster, Inc.
For information about special discounts for bulk purchases, please contact Simon & Schuster Special Sales at 1-866-506-1949 or business@simonandschuster.com.
The Simon & Schuster Speakers Bureau can bring authors to your live event. For more information or to book an event, contact the Simon & Schuster Speakers Bureau at 1-866-248-3049 or visit our website at www.simonspeakers.com.
Also available in a Simon & Schuster Books for Young Readers hardcover edition
Book design by Krista Vossen
The text for this book is set in Adobe Caslon.
Map by Drew Willis
The illustrations for this book are rendered in pen and ink.
Manufactured in the United States of America
0515 OFF
First Simon & Schuster Books for Young Readers paperback edition June 2015
2 4 6 8 10 9 7 5 3 1
The Library of Congress has cataloged the hardcover edition as follows:
Lawson, Jessica.
The actual & truthful adventures of Becky Thatcher / Jessica Lawson.
pages cm
Summary: In 1860, eleven-year-old Becky Thatcher, new to St. Petersburg, Missouri, joins the boys at school in a bet to steal from the Widow Douglas in hopes of meeting a promise to have adventures that she made her brother, Jon, before he died.
ISBN 978-1-4814-0150-0 (hc)
[1. Behavior—Fiction. 2. Adventure and adventurers—Fiction. 3. Family life—Missouri—Fiction. 4. Mississippi River—Fiction. 5. Missouri—History—19th century—Fiction.]
I. Twain, Mark, 1835–1910. Adventures of Tom Sawyer. II. Title. III. Title: Actual and truthful adventures of Becky Thatcher.
PZ7.L438267Act 2014
[Fic]—dc23
2013020560
ISBN 978-1-4814-0153-1 (pbk)
ISBN 978-1-4814-0155-5 (eBook)

FOR MOM, THE WRITER
FOR DAD, THE STORYTELLER

ACKNOWLEDGMENTS

First and foremost, to Samuel Langhorne Clemens, a.k.a. Mark Twain: Thank you, sir. I have the utmost respect and admiration for your work. This story was directly inspired by one of your books and there's no getting around that, but please don't strike me down with some sort of witty, wise, humor-based vengeance from the Great Beyond for leaning heavily on your plot and characters. I am ever grateful for your words.

To my wonderful, tireless, hilarious agent, Tina Wexler: You have provided me with countless words of support and wisdom, and have made me smile more than I can say. Thank you for changing my life, you life-changer you.

To my editor, Kristin Ostby, who I will refer to as *The Manuscript Whisperer*: thank you for your gentle guidance, brilliant ideas, fabulous sense of humor, and generous use of exclamation points in written communication.

To Justin Chanda and the entire team at Simon & Schuster Books for Young Readers: I owe you all so much. Thank you to Krista Vossen for the book's design and to the incomparable Iacopo Bruno for his cover and illustrations.

Thank you to critique partners Joy McCullough-Carranza, Becky Wallace, Tara Dairman, and Ann Bedichek. Emily, Lucia, and Evelyn Paul were the first readers from my target audience and they gave invaluable feedback as well.

Thank you to my husband, Christopher, for giving me time to work and for altering the course of my life by writing me four sonnets (your good looks factored in, but the sonnets clinched it).

Lastly, though the publication of this book is dedicated to my parents, any heart found in the story is for Mimi, Kate, and Sara. And, of course, for Jon.

ST. PETERSBURG, MISSOURI
1860

Chapter One

Caught in the night

My left leg twitched at the tickle of another night-boy. Hidden by the wide trunk of a river sycamore, I shifted in my crouch and reached a hand inside Jon's over-alls to trap and smack the creeping skitter. Darn things had been a considerable nuisance since I settled myself along the Mississippi to have a look-see at the grounded steamboat and its crew.

The men had piled onshore and hauled sitting logs from the brush while I played at them being pirates and me being a stowaway. With the help of passed flasks and a roaring riverside fire, they'd gone from grumbling to mighty spirited in the last hour, and before long I got sucked in by a story one of them was reading from a tablet of writing paper. I was tolerably invested in the tale of a dimwit and his ornery bullwhip—the dimwit having whipped himself nearly to tears while the bull watched—and barely had time to react when the listener nearest me rose with a chuckle and a belch.

While the crew applauded the story's end, I deepened my crouch and slunk farther behind the tree, checking to make sure Jon's marble sack was still stuffed into one of my hip pockets.

The belching man stumbled around the fire with a happy laugh. "You mean to tell us," he said, lurching at the storyteller, "that you put those words together in your own head?"

"That's how writing generally works," the story man said, standing and stretching. "Think up a few lies, put them to paper. I imagine any of you liars would make a fine writer. Now I best get going, boys. I suggest you find lodging in town somewhere." He dusted stray bits of log bark from his pants and sighed. "I'll be staying in a house on Willow Street if you need me. Blue house, black shutters, white porch."

Willow? That was the street we lived on. Forgetting my stowaway role, I backed up and crunched down on an unfortunately placed twig, crying out as the skitter in my overalls came back to life and buzzed around my pant leg. Before I could flee, the storyteller's face was in my own.

"Boys, guard your secrets, we've got a spy." The man gave a once-over to my braids and small stature. "A tricky one, by the looks of her." His smile was amused and friendly, but I knew better than to trust a pirate, even a made-up one.

Swallowing slowly, I stepped into the firelight, showing that I wasn't afraid of dying a dastardly pirate death if that was to be my fate. I gathered my courage to make a real good speech about them never taking me alive, but when I looked over the puzzled crew, it seemed better to keep things brief. "I'm . . .

I'm just out hunting night frogs for fish bait. Guess I'm about done."

The story man winked at me. "Hunting night frogs? I believe *you'd* make a decent writer too. You're out mighty late. Care for a nightcap?" He held out a flask, then pulled it back with a grin. "No, you better not. You need someone to walk you home, Miss?"

I lit out for home without answering, cursing skitters in general and the one who'd made a feast outta my leg in particular. And twigs. I cursed them plenty as well.

The riverbank gave way to a dirt road, cool and smooth under my bare feet with barely a pebble to throw. Only a town as boring as a bible lesson would have such clean dirt roads. When I breathed in through my nose, lingering wood smoke from the crew's fire mixed with the early autumn scent of dry, sunbaked grass and ripening leaves. I stood still for a second in the light of the stars and waxing moon, wriggling my toes and taking a look at my new life. The night version of St. Petersburg spread out before me in a quiet beauty that was too calm for my taste. Too much like a place that had never gotten to know my brother.

Once I was in our yard, I avoided the Miss Ada–shaped shadow in the lamplit kitchen and scooted around the house. I lifted the parlor window. *Well, shoot.* That tiny squeaking sound wasn't bad, but somebody went and put clinky vases on the table next to the window, and *somebody* went and parked her body in the parlor and fell asleep.

Ducking behind Mama's big blue armchair, I timed my movement with her snoring and snuck a look at her nightly reading, which she'd forgotten on the end table. Looked like some muckety-muck romance book to me. Tucked in her hand was the family portrait that I hadn't seen since she hid it away a year ago. In the photograph, Daddy looked stern and handsome and Mama was soft-smiled and pretty. Jon looked straight into the camera, his eye twinkle standing out even in black and white. My face was covered up by Mama's sleeping fingers. Gently moving her hand so I was back in the family, I gave my mama a good long stare, soaking up the sight of her looking peaceful instead of sad.

Then, ever so careful, I tippy-toed across the parlor while Mama snored on. It wasn't until I reached my room and closed the door, quiet as a tinkle in the woods, that I saw him.

Daddy.

Judge Thatcher, as I called him when I got into mischief, was sitting on my bed with his arms crossed. In one hand was his fancy pocket watch, the one he used in court matters. About the size of a baby's palm, it was always shiny and always wound and *always* exactly on time. He called it Old Reliable. Me and Old Reliable weren't on friendly terms.

"It's past ten o'clock, Becky," he said, snapping the watch shut. When he caught sight of my clothing, I saw him soften and go to a sorrowful place before he recovered himself. "Mighty late, considering you said your good nights nearly two hours ago."

"Oh, is it late?" I asked. "Well, I guess I'll get to sleep." I yawned real big. "Judge, I'll have to ask you to excuse yourself. I'm getting mighty big to have my daddy stick around to sing a lullaby, so feel free to get on to bed. You look real tired."

"I believe you can spare a moment or two." He caught my nose between a giant finger and thumb and squeezed it nice and playful, but his eyes looked like business. "Are you going to be giving me trouble every night, Miss Becky?" He said it in his low, low voice that sounded like molasses would, if molasses could talk. When he added a gravelly rumble and stood to his full height of over six feet, he could make criminals shake in their stolen boots.

"No, sir, I won't be giving you trouble every night." *And I wouldn't be any trouble at all if you'd quit waiting up to catch me.*

He patted the bed for me to sit down. "We're trying for a fresh start here. I have enough on my mind between making sure your mama settles in and having the Pritchard brothers loose in my jurisdiction. Is that understood? Eleven-year-old girls belong in bed, not exploring a town like it was a new territory."

"It's new territory to me," I said.

"Becky . . ." He trailed off, but the tone of his voice said plenty more.

"Who are the Pritchard brothers?" Asking Daddy about work usually got him good and distracted. I put on a fearful face and added a tremble to my voice. "Are they awful dangerous?"

"Hard to say. The location says they like to thieve and cause trouble. They've gone missing upriver and that's reason enough for you to not be sneaking around at night. No more of your wildness, you hear?"

Hmm. It seemed mighty convenient to have marauders about when the Judge didn't want me wandering. I half-wondered if Daddy hadn't made them up on the spot. "Yes, sir."

"Hold out your fingers, so I can see you aren't crossing them."

Well, shoot. He couldn't see my feet, though.

"Toes, too, you rascal." He smiled and I thought I was off the hook for sure, but the grin was followed by one of those big adult sighs, like a girl having a little adventure was about the heaviest thing in the world, and it was sitting right on my daddy's shoulder, weighing him down with a terrible pressure. "Don't you want to know how you got caught?"

I considered the question for traps and additional punishment, then gave a hesitant nod. "Yes, Judge."

"A boy about your age was down the street, doing school-work on his front porch around eight thirty this evening."

I cursed myself for not wearing a hat to tuck my hair out of sight. "Must not be the brightest of boys," I noted. "I always have mine done before supper."

Daddy flinched like he'd been skitter-bit. "Maybe he's more vexed by schoolwork than you. Anyhow, this boy saw you pass down the street alone and told his aunt."

I reached around my brain, hunting for cover. "Could've been anyone that he saw. Could've been a dog."

Daddy gave me his staring-down-at-a-criminal expression. "Becky, we've been seen around town for a few days now. He recognized you, and his aunt sent him over in case we didn't know your whereabouts. Mighty uncomfortable thing to happen. What in Lord's name were you doing?"

I shrugged. "Nothing worth telling anyone's aunt about. I was checking on that grounded steamboat. Heard it let out a blast and went to investigate. I wanted to make sure it didn't go crazy and blow up the whole town. How's that wrong?"

"Becky . . ."

I held up one hand, just like I was testifying in court. "Judge, I solemnly swear that I couldn't help it. There's something real mysterious about a steamboat at night. All sorts of people were sitting around a fire right there by the river."

"Oh, Becky." He shook his head at me and rubbed his big hands up and down his face. "Tell me, how did you ever manage to pull yourself away from that scene?"

"Got caught listening. They offered me some of their liquor, and I didn't take any," I relayed, hoping to earn some goody points. "Then I ran home."

He sighed another big one and sifted both hands through his hair. He oughtn't do that. Mama says he doesn't have much more hair to lose, without him helping it along like that. That is, she used to say that, back when she was being Mama.

"Becky, you've got a good heart, but you've also got more excuses than common sense. It wouldn't hurt you to make some attempt to grow up. It's time to show me you know what it means to be responsible."

Well, it took most of my strength not to stick my tongue out at that business.

"Get to bed. And stop wearing your brother's clothes, all right? I can take it, but it gives your mama a considerable amount of heartache to see you in Jon's overalls and shirts. It's hardly been a year."

I knew how long it'd been, of course. A year had come and gone last month, and that's when Daddy decided it was time for us to move. Probably on account of something to do with Mama's sadness that I couldn't get any particulars on, other than I was supposed to keep my mouth shut tight about matters that didn't concern me. And that wasn't anything I hadn't heard a sackful of times already. "Yes, Judge Thatcher."

He placed a kiss on each of my black braids. "I reckon I'm back to being Daddy." He walked to the door and blew me a third kiss.

"Yes, Daddy. And Daddy?"

He paused. "Yes, sweetheart?"

"What was that boy's name? The one that told on me."

Daddy scratched his head and yawned. "I believe his name was Thomas Sawyer. Looked about your age. Most likely, you'll meet him at school tomorrow."

After hearing Daddy's footsteps fade down the stairs, I took my sack of special marbles from my pocket and held them tight as I said my prayers, telling that writer man's story to Jon up in Heaven. I heard his laughter in my head, which made me feel good and cozy and safe.

"Don't you worry, Jon. I'll find a way to keep my promise." I gave the marbles a little hug. *I miss you so much my toes ache*, I added to myself, not wanting to share that particular thought with my brother. Jon had always been too full of spirit to bother with sadness.

Then I said my good night to the world and commenced to sleeping my last sleep before my first day of school in St. Petersburg, Missouri. It was a shame, but most likely I would not have a kind word for that Sawyer boy when I met him.

Darn that Tom.

Chapter Two

———— ◆ ————

Ugly outlaws and the town witch
and a sore eye

There's not much better in the world than waking up to hotcakes and sausage cooking. I smelled it even as I was coming out of my sleep, so I got up happy. Splashed my face and washed my legs off, wrestled my tights on without tearing them, combed and braided my mop, and got on my blue dress with the horrible lace collar. That sausage smelled so fine that I barely cringed while doing up my buttons.

Sliding into a seat at the small table in the kitchen, I breathed in the delicious aroma and promise of maple syrup. Even though the room was a long rectangle instead of the square of our old kitchen, our wall-plates hung on display and so did the familiar chalkboard where Miss Ada wrote down the dinner menu. Fried chicken and corn and taters and peach pie, it said. If I closed my eyes and inhaled, it almost felt like we were back in Riley. And if I squeezed them real tight, I could almost imagine that Jon was just late to the morning meal.

Miss Ada was at the stove, flipping the meat patties so they flew in the air, whipped around, and slapped back down. Then she seared them with a hot sizzle. I loved that sound. She wouldn't let me help ever since I flipped one straight up to the ceiling, where it left an awful grease mark.

"Don't you let me catch you drinking out of that syrup jug, Miss Becky," she said, not taking her eyes off the pan. "Breakfast'll be right along."

Dropping my fingers from the handle, I dipped my pinky finger far inside the half-full jug and came up with nothing. Darn it. "Yes, Miss Ada."

She was all bustling arms with a string-bean frame and meant business most of the time, though she'd smiled at me more since Jon died. She always smelled like hotcakes and soap, which was a nice sort of smell. Miss Ada'd been with us since I was just a year old and she was fourteen. I was awful glad when she agreed to move with us even though it meant moving to a slave-keeping state. Her small cabin was out in the back garden, and I wondered what she did in there during her free time.

"Y'all ready for school, sugar?" She rubbed her left arm where the fat had jumped out of the pan and bit her.

I couldn't bring myself to answer. *School.* I must've known I'd be going, since I got dressed up like a store doll, but I confess it was a disappointment to hear the word out loud. Then I remembered that I would be meeting that big fat tattletale, Thomas Sawyer. I'd have to think on a nice punishment for that boy. Maybe a little maple stickiness on his desk seat would fix him right. But, no, somebody was sure to miss the jug if I snuck it to school.

Miss Ada turned and smiled at me, brown lips turned up like sunny sausage links. "Who are you over there? Couldn't be Miss Becky Thatcher. This girl in front of me looks scrubbed and sharp as a needle. You even got your coonskin on," she said with a wink and a tug on my dress sleeve.

"Fishskin, Miss Ada," I grumbled. I had a special kind of dislike for dresses and called them my fishskins. When I was wearing one, I felt like a fish caught in a net and could barely keep from jerking and jiggling. "Better make it three cakes today."

"'Scuse me?"

"Please, Miss Ada."

"That's right, *please*," she said, scooting four steaming cakes onto my plate. She slid the butter dish toward me and made up a plate for Mama, who'd been taking her meals upstairs. "Your mama may not be talking much lately, but even she keeps her manners. She'd want you doing the same."

It didn't seem real good manners to me to read books with titles like *Woe Betide the Dangerous Inclinations of a Soldier's Wife's Heart.* "Miss Ada, why do you reckon Mama likes spending time with those romantical books of hers?"

Snatching the syrup jug off the table, Miss Ada sighed at my plate. "You're gonna make yourself sick with all that sugar. I don't know why she likes those books. Maybe 'cause she can skip the bad parts. Can't do that in life."

"Oh." I made quick work of half the hotcakes and drowned my sausage in syrup, playing at letting it struggle before it went dead enough for me to eat. *Not a nice game,* Jon used to say, *but it sure makes sitting at a breakfast table more tolerable.* "Why do you reckon she hides that photograph of the family?"

Miss Ada shook her head. "Misses that piece of her life, maybe. Wants it back and doesn't know what to do about it. Terrible thing about your brother, Miss Becky, but folks got to make the best of whatever mess gets spilled on them."

I wasn't sure if Miss Ada meant that Jon's death was the mess that got spilled on us, or if I was the mess left behind. "Is she gonna be sad forever?"

Miss Ada shrugged. "Maybe not. Hope not." She patted my head. "I heard some gossip at the store yesterday and thought you might like to know. That grounded steamboat's engine is all spoiled up and they had to send upriver for new parts. Could be stuck here for two weeks or so," she said.

My goodness. A whole steamboat sitting there for two weeks, just waiting to be explored.

"Now, Miss Becky, you *git* that look out your eye! I declare, you're as bad as poor Jon was at your age."

I fixed a guilty expression on my face, but inside, I felt proud. Wasn't a bigger compliment in the world to me. I smothered the last sausage and popped it in my mouth, giving a glance toward the staircase. "I'm leaving, Mama," I mumbled, my words too soft and food filled for Miss Ada to take notice. I handed my plate over.

She took the dish, placing a patchwork-fabric lunch sack in my hand. "You know where the schoolhouse is?"

"Yes, Miss Ada." Straightening my posture so I looked good and grown-up, I stepped into Daddy's home office to say good-bye. My eye caught on a poster sitting on his desk. Daddy was nowhere to be seen, so I let my shoulders drop and roll into a hunch while I leaned forward to read.

WANTED: 2 PRITCHARDS
(Billy and Forney)

Wanted for train robbery, bank robbery, and possible murder.

Description:
Billy Pritchard~near 6 foot tall.
Forney Pritchard~considerably shorter.

Few teeth, longish dark hair, fondness for liquor and tobacco. Generally filthy.

Reward for information leading directly to arrests.

If the likenesses were right, they were the ugliest men I'd ever seen. Daddy hadn't mentioned the possible murder bit, which made the Pritchards a heap more scary and, therefore, more interesting.

Sticking the lunch sack in my leather school satchel, I checked for my pencil case and marbles, then scooted out the back door.

St. Petersburg was pushed right up against the west bank of the Mississippi River, and town was mostly laid out like the chessboard in Daddy's office. It was a big change from living on the outskirts of Riley, where activity centered around the busy downtown and railroad depot.

This tree-filled town seemed slow and sleepy from the moment we'd stepped from the *Duchess Daisy* three days earlier. At that time, a cargo steamboat was docked in front of us, unloading goods from St. Louis and getting loaded back up with logs from the sawmill. Other than the mill, there wasn't much to town except a dry-goods store, a café, a tailoring shop, a butcher shop, a couple of liveries, and an empty jail. Daddy said it'd be real peaceful here. He said it'd make for an easy job of being town Judge and be good for Mama, too. It was a worrisome thing to be so surrounded by peacefulness when the marble promise I'd made to Jon required a good amount of adventuring. Still, the distant threat of two outlaws and a whole big river promised to keep life interesting.

One block from my house, a boy about my age jumped from his porch. With an easy stroll, hands parked in a pair of suspenders, he pulled alongside me on the sidewalk. He looked so sharp in his black pants and ironed shirt, I might have been intimidated if he weren't barefoot, shoes tied to his book strap. I wiggled all ten toes inside my brown saddle shoes. There wasn't much wiggling room in there.

That boy had nice black curls and smiled like he knew me. When I gave a hesitant smile back, he stuck one hand out and used the other to tip his straw hat. The sun was getting higher in the sky, and it lit up his hair in a fancy glow. Mama used to say angel glow was surrounding me when I got hit by sunlight like that. These days I doubted she'd notice if my head caught on fire.

"Sid Sawyer, here." His grin was wide and gap-toothed.

Sawyer? Looking past Sid, I saw a nice blue two-story with a wide yard cut off from view by a shabby-looking fence. I scanned the property for any sign of the tattletale, but the only other soul there was too old for school. Right on the wrap-around porch sat the writer fellow I'd seen the night before. He sipped from a steaming cup, reading a paper and looking like he had a headache. "Who's that?" I asked, pointing to the rocking chair.

"That?" Sid scratched a red spot on his cheek, left by a skitter or spider. "That's Sam Clemens. He's the riverboat pilot from that grounded steamboat. Said he got kicked off his passenger boat job for being ornery so they switched him over to a shipping boat for a few weeks to teach him a lesson. He's waiting on a part to come in."

"What's he gonna do while he waits?"

Sid shrugged. "Says he's gonna read a little and write a little and do a little of nothing at all. Says there's plenty to catch the eye around here, but I suspect he'll be disappointed. Anyway, I already know who you are." He did a whistly song, going real high.

It was a darn impressive whistle, and he didn't look all impressed with himself, just happy, so that was something. Plus, I was willing to bet that gap tooth was mighty fine for spitting. Still, I didn't like it when people knew things about me, especially when I didn't know a thing about them, except that they were a better whistler and their fence could use a whitewashing.

"Oh? Who am I, then?"

"You're Judge Thatcher's daughter. Becky, right? As for me, I belong to my aunt. She's older than dirt, but nice enough."

The tattler had spoken to an aunt. "You related to Thomas Sawyer?"

"Sure I am. Tom is my half-brother. He saw you sneaking down the road last night. Where'd you go?"

I narrowed my eyes and ignored the question, taking another look at their porch and trying to figure out where that Tom had been sitting when he saw me. "Where is that brother of yours?" I asked.

"*Half*-brother," Sid said. "And not a ripe half neither."

"How come he's only a half?"

Sid dug at his lower teeth with a fingernail and wiped whatever he'd come up with on the nearest tree. "My daddy got horsekicked when I was only a year old, then Mama got married again and had Tom. Then she died too."

"Bet you miss them."

He shrugged. "Never got to know them, so they're hard ones to miss. I was just two and Tom was still crawling on the floor. But there's better things to talk about than my corn cob of a brother." Sid paused at the street corner. He pointed back toward the river a couple of blocks. A lone house stood there, brown and sturdy, made of clapboard. It had a wrap-around porch and a big crabapple tree in the front yard. Early pumpkins and gourds bordered a side garden where an oldish woman stooped over a bed of flowers. Beside her was a set of worn gardens tools—shovel, rake, and hoe. The tip of every handle was painted red.

"Now *there's* something you outta know about. See her?" Sid pointed again and jabbed me twice with his knuckles. "That lady. Do you see her?"

My arm got a little sore from the knuckle jab, but I held off rubbing. "I got eyes, don't I?"

"She's a witch," he declared. "The Widow Douglas is her name, but she's a witch for certain. See those pumpkins? Each one is a boy or girl she's stolen. Turns their heads into pumpkins and gourds and sets them out so all the bad spirits are sure to find her."

Peering closer, I saw that there must've been at least ten stolen heads around that garden. You would think she'd have been strung up and hanged for that level of witchery. "Don't people get mad? Where's she steal them all from?"

Sid waved a hand vaguely. "Probably a big city upriver. Chicago, maybe. They got so many people up there, folks'd hardly notice a few missing." He looked at me, most likely waiting for me to shiver or let out a fearful moan.

Instead I shrugged. Jon always said fear was like a cake cooling in the window. If you happen to stumble upon some you should keep it to yourself instead of sharing it around. "Shame for those who get snatched, but I reckon we're safe enough."

Sid scowled plenty. "I reckon we're *not*. See her red-tipped tools? Might as well be a devil's pitchfork in that mix. She's always outside with her crazy weeds and herbs." He stared at me again, jutting his chin out for good measure. "*Evil* weeds and herbs. For her spells, I imagine."

I squinted at the herbs. One looked like lavender to me. And I saw a bunch of mint for certain. Miss Ada says it spreads like gossip. But I knew it wasn't polite to argue too much when a new friend is pointing out the town witch. Besides, those red-tipped tools *were* a dead giveaway. Everyone knew red was a devil color unless it was on clothes, strawberry jam, the American flag, or Christmas decorations.

"Anyway," Sid said, "stare too long at her front door and your eyeballs pop right out and then you turn into a pig. Plus, her big hound is voodoo cursed. She can put her soul into him. You'll see him wandering around town late at night, but really it's her." He put his hands in those suspenders and whapped them against his chest, glancing at me sideways. "Us boys got near five dollars in the pot for whoever steals something from inside the house. Reckon we'll be trying real soon."

He made a left toward school, whistling again. I caught up with a little skipping that I reined in before Sid saw. Jon always said to keep my fishskin skipping for when I was with girls. Boys don't like to be around skirt-tossing skips and giggles, he'd say. "What do you have to steal for the bet?" I asked. "Spells and such?"

I had only one true experience with spells and witchy folk back in Riley. My armpits started trickling just thinking about it. Still, five dollars was a good amount of money, I was awful fond of winning bets, and Jon would have *loved* the sound of this one. As long as I had his marbles on me, it was my responsibility to treat them to some worthy adventures. Witches and gambling seemed like a good start.

"Any proof that you been inside," Sid said. "Dead man's toes, jar of cursed warts. Whatever witchiness is handy."

"Is Tom doing the bet?"

"No, he's too yellow and prissy. Ho, now!" Sid gave me a good shove, his eyebrows near jumping into his hair. "Get moving," he hissed, tilting his head at the Widow's house. "She's *watching*."

Sure enough, the Widow had noticed us whispering and stood straight up, shovel in hand, facing our way. Once both of us were staring, her free hand did a wiggle in the air and then pointed straight at our hearts!

"Go!" I squeaked, and we both took off.

He paused two blocks from the dirt path that led off the road to the schoolhouse and caught his breath. "Good thing Tom wasn't with us. He would've wet his pants for sure." Sid smiled and leaned closer. "He wet his pants only last year. Had too much lemonade during the school picnic up on the high meadow over thataway. Did it near the old cave, away from all the hoo-ha, but did it all the same."

I nodded, still breathing hard. Pants wetting was good information to have. I tried to think if I had anything to trade back. "Couple of outlaws went missing upriver a ways. Daddy says they might be heading downriver to town. Thieves and murderers."

Sid gave an appreciative whistle and kept walking. "Murderers is good. Say, go 'head and tell where you went last night, won't you?"

"Snuck down to check on that grounded steamboat and saw a bunch of men sitting around a fire. That man staying with you was telling stories he wrote himself while they all drank *whiskey*." I watched for a reaction and was pleased to see he was paying close attention when I mentioned such a forbidden thing as whiskey. "Got offered some."

Sid stopped again outside a real pretty white house with a proper-painted fence. He licked his lips, and looked kinda nervous and kinda hopeful. "You take it?"

"Naw, depending on the kind, it might burn a hole in my stomach, since I'm not grown."

He looked relieved and nodded. "I heard that too. Otherwise I'd try some just about anytime."

The dirt path to the school was only ten yards off, and I could see the red building tucked into the trees. My dress started feeling even tighter around the neck, when something hit me right in the eye. My head snapped back and I couldn't help but let out a small shriek (just a small one, I reckon) because it hurt so and came out of nowhere.

I clutched the busted eye with two hands, trying to press the stabbing pain back where it came from. In all my shuffling about, I must've stomped right on one of Sid's bare feet, because he howled like a wolf. I squinted my good eye open in time to see that he'd dropped to a knee right in front of me. Before I could stop moving forward, my legs slammed into his bent body, and I flew right over and tumbled.

Good Lord, then there was a terrible, awful bang on my knee, and I near passed out trying to decide whether or not to take a hand from my dangling eyeball in order to check that my knee was still there. Also, to pull my dress back down over my rear end.

"Move! Move aside!" A shadow swept over me, and the smell of flowers followed. "What on earth is going on here! Sid Sawyer, what have you done! Oh, you poor thing!"

"I think my eye's out," I whispered, my hands still plastered to my face. "I can feel the blood."

"Sid, you run in and get a wet cloth," a kindly voice said. I felt a gentle hand on my back as a rush of boys' voices beat around me.

"It was this ball!"

"He got her right in the face!"

"Danny Boggs did it!"

The kind voice grew firm as it interrupted. "Daniel Boggs, did you throw that ball?"

"It was an accident," a boy mumbled.

"Boys, just clear out! Clear out and get to school. Let me get a look at this eye. Give me that cloth, Sid."

Soft hands pried my fingers away, and I braced myself for the kind woman to gasp and faint. It was to be expected, with my eye dangling like a piece of fish bait.

"Well, honey, it's not bad at all. The ball was made out of knitting yarn. It was tightly wound, but knitting yarn nonetheless." She dabbed at my eyes with the cloth. "I suspect you'll be fine. There's no blood, just some tears from your eye watering."

Knitting yarn? *Well, shoot.* I sat up and blinked. More water came out, but she was right. My eyeball was firmly in its socket, and I was late for school.

"I'm Mrs. Sprague, the preacher's wife, honey. I stopped by the day you all arrived to have a visit with your mama, but your daddy said she was feeling poorly. And you're Becky, isn't that right? I saw you at church yesterday morning. Your mama must still be sick, her missing the service."

She'll be missing more, I wanted to say, but I didn't think Mrs. Sprague would want to hear about my mama not being on friendly terms with the Lord, not to mention other people. She looked too nice with her poufy blond bun and her blue-and-white checked dress, and I didn't want to mess up her pretty face by making it frown. "Yes, ma'am, she's still getting over a cold."

"Well, I know how that is. Are you feeling fine to go on to school?"

"I'm all right, ma'am." I struggled to my feet, a little embarrassed. The pain seemed to have disappeared along with my horrible eye injury. I felt a tickle on my shin, prepared to slap the offending skitter, and lit up when I saw torn tights and a beauty of a knee cut.

"Oh!" cried Mrs. Sprague. "Look at that knee! There's some blood there, honey. Come on inside so you can take those tights off. I'm afraid they're too torn for mending, but you'll be fine without them. Sid, you wait here to walk her to school and explain to Mr. Dobbins. I know how strict he can be with being on time."

Sid waited while I limped inside. The house was like a museum of badly crocheted doilies. Small ones were tucked under table candles and a large one was draped over the plum-colored parlor sofa. Too many to count were strung on the walls. I liked Mrs. Sprague even more because those doilies were so awful looking. It showed that even preachers' wives had flaws.

We left the house with another cloth and some bandages and a paper bag that smelled like rapture itself. "Those are for being so brave, dear," she said, squeezing my shoulder. "I'm sure Danny Boggs didn't mean to hit you."

I nodded. *Danny Boggs, Danny Boggs,* I committed to memory. Now I had two boys on my list of people to get some vengeance on.

"I'm glad he owned to it," Mrs. Sprague said. "His daddy may go easier on him for that." She tilted my chin up with a gentle smile and studied my eye. "Makes me think of John 8:32."

"Jon who?"

"It's a Bible verse, dear. John 8:32 says that the truth will set you free."

"Yes, ma'am," I said, thinking two things. First, that instead of setting him free, the truth would most likely get Danny Boggs a whipping or scolding at home. Second, I guessed that my brother Jon and the Bible's John probably wouldn't be friends up in Heaven, having different opinions on what sorts of things made a person feel free.

After thanking Mrs. Sprague for the bag of goodies, Sid and I hurried to the schoolhouse, taking turns peeking inside the mystery bag. Inside were four sugar cookies, fresh from the oven and dotting the bag with a little baking grease.

"Reckon you'll share?" he asked, pulling open the schoolhouse door.

"Sure I will. Wasn't your fault about the ball," I told him, taking a deep breath before stepping inside. "Sorry about your foot."

"Sorry about your eye and knee. That'll give you a real nice scab, though."

I grinned. That was something. I did like a good scab to pick at. Plus, it was a good reminder that I didn't ever want to grow up and turn into a responsible young lady. Responsible young ladies didn't pick scabs and they didn't sign up for bets about the town witch.

I'd be doing both.

Chapter Three

———•———

A rat-faced teacher, a pinchy-faced toad, and a bosom friend

The schoolhouse smelled like mold and sweat and felt a month or two hotter than mid-September, despite all the windows being open for air. Stepping inside made me feel like I'd just been squeezed into another dress. Five rows of eight small desks were mostly filled with students quietly talking, their backs to me and Sid. I couldn't rightly tell, but the size of folks seemed to range from about age six to fourteen or so.

"Where's your brother?" I whispered.

Sid pointed. "Half-brother. There he is."

Tom was sitting two rows from the teacher's desk and the big front chalkboard. He was red-necked from the back. Most likely he'd given himself a nice school-day scrubbing. Even from behind, that boy looked like a tattletale, from the way he sat stiff as a board to the cowlick sticking up on his poop-brown hair.

Through a window on the left, I saw a short man walking toward the back door of the schoolhouse with a newspaper under his arm. His ugly tweed jacket was the color of a fungus that sprouted on my foot last summer.

"Dob-head," Sid confirmed. "Coming back from the out-house, like every morning."

Mr. Dobbins's head was a rat-shaped thing. Instead of just his huge nose pointing out, all his features kind of jutted forward, like they were trying to get away from him. Slicked-down black hair topped his head and fell past his ears. He marched inside and slapped his hand on a girl's desk. "Mary Green, you go and ring the late bell."

"I'm Alice," said the girl. "That's Mary." She pointed to an identical sister across the room.

"Just go."

Alice Green scampered out the door as Sid scooted into an empty seat behind his brother. Unsure if I had an assigned seat, I felt I had no choice but to go stand near Mr. Dobbins until he gave me instruction as to where I needed to plant myself. But instead of telling me where to sit, he ignored me and walked over to the coal stove. He sifted through the bucket that held the fire tools.

"Need help starting a fire, sir?" Tom asked, rising slightly from his seat.

Mr. Dobbins snorted. "It's hot as hellfire in here, Tom. You really think I'm about to start a fire?"

Tom sank back down amid muffled taunting, and I nearly

felt bad that even the person he was sucking up to didn't pay him any mind. Then I remembered that I owed him a lick or two.

It looked like Mr. Dobbins was thinking about handing out licks as well. Leaning beside all sorts of sharp, pokey fire things was another pokey thing. It looked to be a good-size hickory switch. He wouldn't switch girls, would he? Especially not girls with bleeding knees and a sore eye.

"Sid Sawyer, join me up front, won't you?"

"Yes, sir."

The room murmured while he got up (flicking his brother on the ear first, I was pleased to see). When Sid reached the front of the classroom, Mr. Dobbins seemed to notice me for the first time. He shot me a real irritable look, like I was a fly or something he found upside his fat nostrils.

The bell rang out four times.

"You must be the new girl," he said. He looked over my shoulder. "Thank you, Miss Green. You may sit down." His beady eyes returned to me and Sid. "I *hate* to make an example of you, but that was the late bell, and you two are the only ones out of your seats."

"What about Alice?" I pointed out.

"Don't you be smart in my schoolhouse. She was outside on my doing." He had a real slimy look on his face. "This being your first day, I simply can't abide by you being late. You're already a week late to the school year, so I take this negligence as a particular and personal insult. And, as this is Sid's third offense, he's due for a triple thwap. Sid and . . ." He looked at me.

"Becky Thatcher," I mumbled.

His eyes lit up, the meanie. "Why, that's right. Becky Thatcher, daughter of our new Judge. I would think the daughter of a town official might have a little more respect for authority." He leaned down, revealing a large set of gums and not-so-sweet breath. "Tell me, did they use a hickory or a ruler on girls where you're from?"

Neither, you weasel-faced grease head. If I were Jon, I would've been clear to the river by now. Unfortunately, though, I wasn't Jon and I could see that my new teacher aimed to punish me unless I could give him a reason not to. "Mr. Dobbins," I said in a steady voice, "it wasn't our fault we were late. You see, this ball came out of nowhere, and—"

That mean old teacher put his finger right in my face. "Playing ball on the way to school? And you want to be excused?"

Desperately scanning the faces of the classroom, I searched for a savior. But they all looked away or put their heads down. "Sir, I—"

He held a hand up and sniffed the air. "And are those *cookies*?" He snatched the paper bag from my hand and stuck his fat red nose right in it, then opened the bottom drawer of his desk and shoved them inside. Sid let out a little whimper of disappointment, and I knew those cookies were lost for good.

"I don't know how they do things over there where you're from, Miss Thatcher," Mr. Dobbins continued, "but you're in St. Petersburg now. If you insist on talking back, I do believe I'll recommend that you miss the annual picnic next month."

There was a collective gasp around the classroom, and I felt the threat slam into me. The picnic was likely a most-sought-after place to be, especially if there were embarrassments to be seen like Tom Sawyer peeing himself. I *couldn't* miss it.

"I am *not* talking back, sir."

"Enough, young lady. Stick out your wrist." His index finger tapped the hickory twice before he set it down and dug through his top desk drawer, coming up with a flat wooden stick. "Girls get the ruler," he said, smiling.

Good Lord, that man was about to strike me!

Sid finally got the frog outta his throat and spoke up. "Mr. Dobbins, she's right about us having a good reason, sir."

"And you, Sid Sawyer, can bend over. You'll be next."

I watched, terrified. Just as Mr. Dobbins was raising the ruler above my wrist, one of the cowards proved himself otherwise.

"What *are* you waving your hand for, Daniel Boggs?"

"She . . . well, she fell on the way to school. Preacher's wife helped her out and made Sid wait for her, and that's why they're late. Mrs. Sprague will tell you. I believe she's become partial to Becky."

Thank you, Danny Boggs. I no longer aim to hit you with a rock during the lunch break.

Mr. Dobbins seemed to have himself a head battle between Mrs. Sprague's partialness and the satisfaction he'd get from smacking me a good one. After a long moment, he put away the ruler. "It's bad form to cross a preacher's wife, I suppose." With a disappointed sigh, he walked the switch back to the corner. "Get back to your desk," he said to Sid. "Take a seat, Miss Thatcher. Your book will be under the desk lid."

I could hardly breathe after that business. We'd been set

free from punishment, but it was Mrs. Sprague's name, not the truth, that had done it. Mr. Dobbins hadn't given a rat's tail about truth when I'd told it to him. Maybe that's why Jon usually lied his way into lesser punishments when Mama and Daddy caught him in a piece of mischief. I tapped my satchel pocket, feeling the outline of the marbles while making a mental note to be wary of the trouble that came from being honest with grown-ups.

"How do I know where to sit, sir?" I made sure to ask real polite, and even turned my toes out, which was straight from the Bible, I was pretty sure.

"Try a spot where nobody is, Miss Thatcher. The spots with people in them are mighty inconvenient to learning."

I felt my face go hot while the boys in class snickered and the girls covered their mouths with their hands to hide smiles. "I hate you," I mumbled.

"What, Miss Thatcher?"

"Thank you," I said, sliding into a seat behind Sid.

Mr. Dobbins straightened his horrible jacket and paced around the room, looking for someone to embarrass. "Today we're doing spelling. How many of you know how to spell the word 'knee'? Rose Hobart, how about you?"

A petite girl with a brown braid down to her waist stood and cleared her throat. "Knee. *N-E . . . E.*"

"*Wrong*," Dobbins said. He pointed to two students. "You next, then you when he gets it wrong."

Two more boys misspelled "*knee*" before a nice-looking girl stood and gave it a try. She was in my row, all the way over to the right.

"That's correct, Amy," Mr. Dobbins said in a real snotty voice. "I must say, you've got excellent spelling skills for being the daughter of the town drunk."

Immediately, I felt real bad for her. I knew what it was like to be stuck in a box because of who your daddy was.

Two seats in front of me, Tom Sawyer gave a nervous twittery chuckle at Mr. Dobbins's mean words, like he wasn't sure if it was a joke that required someone to acknowledge it. Nobody joined him, though, which meant he alone was laughing at that Amy girl.

I wadded up a tiny piece of paper and wet it with my tongue the way Jon had showed me, then tucked my index finger around it. Raising my hand to my mouth real casual, I leaned to the left to avoid Sid and made it look like maybe I was just scratching my chin while I took in a solid breath and blew hard.

I got Tom Sawyer right on the ear. He howled like that tiny wad of paper was the sharpest thing in the world. It was so satisfying that I made a note to search for a stinkbug to put in his desk. The spitball was for that girl. I still owed Tom Sawyer for tattling on me.

I must've let a laugh escape, because Amy leaned forward and smiled at me, kinda shy. She had wonderful auburn hair, part red and part brown, and it was brushed ever so nice and pulled half back with a green ribbon. I smiled back.

Then she did something that made me like her an awful lot. She winked at me, and stuck her tongue in Tom Sawyer's direction.

The sticking-out tongue made me think that maybe, just

maybe, she was the kind of girl who would partner up with me to take on Sid's witchy bet.

Jon, I think I found a friend.

By lunchtime I was missing those cookies something awful, but I saw Dobbins lock his desk drawer with a fancy key before he left for the outhouse. Boys and girls filed outside and found themselves cool spots under shade trees or at a few picnic tables. Tom Sawyer shuffled around his brother's group of friends until they shooed him off with jeers and a few well-aimed pebbles.

Sid smiled and gestured me over, but I thought it best to try to sit with girls. Miss Ada and Mama would say that was the right thing to do, and I really didn't want to make Daddy look bad by being too friendly with boys. It was hard, though, because those boys had cards out, and I do love a game of cards.

Three girls sat at a table that had an open space on one side. Two of them were the Green twins, who looked exactly alike down to their matching sunbonnets. They sat across from a beanpole of a girl whose yellow hair was done in two braids like mine. She had blue ribbons at the ends of hers. My mind drifted to the dresser at home, where I'd left two good white ribbons. Didn't wear them, because I didn't want to seem too fancy.

Darn if I didn't wish I had those ribbons in my hair now.

Taking a deep breath, I walked over only to have the beanpole girl scoot her behind to block me.

"Seat's taken," she stated matter-of-factly.

I recognized her from church the day before. She'd worn

a white embroidered frock and shiny black dress shoes. With her thin scowly lips and all her features squished together, she looked just like a pinchy-faced toad I caught on Jon's fishing pole once. Her mother was a bigger version of toad and had spoken nicely to Daddy before glaring at my church shoes, which were the opposite of shiny.

One of the twins looked at the behind-scooting girl. "Seat's taken by who, Ruth? Nobody was sitting there."

Ruth ignored her and jabbed a finger toward the stream. "Why don't you go sit with Amy Lawrence? Her daddy being the town drunk and your daddy being the town judge, you're bound to run into each other soon enough." She smiled sweetly, but her eyes stayed as mean as a trapped raccoon. "Oh, and her mama's dead and I hear your brother's dead, so you can talk about dead people too."

My face got hot at that business. "I do believe you've earned a spot on my special list," I told her.

Her pinchy eyes turned to squinty slits. "What list is that?"

"I reckon you'll find out," I said, raising my eyebrows with a hint of mysteriousness. Jon would've been proud that I used his favorite threat.

I gripped my satchel and walked close to where Amy sat under a trio of cottonwoods. I was determined to be friendly and make her like me as much as I liked her. Amy Lawrence was mourning a family death too. Between that and our mutual dislike for Tom Sawyer and Mr. Dobbins, I was becoming more and more certain of our destiny to be great friends and partners for the witchy bet.

Settling my nerves, Amy brightened at my approach and

patted the ground next to her. "I've been hoping you'd come sit with me. I've liked you since you shot that spitball at Tom Sawyer."

"You have?" That warmed me up like a sunrise. There isn't hardly anything more nice than someone telling you they like you for who you are. "I saw you stick your tongue out. That was risky."

"I don't care. Mr. Dobbins is . . ."

"He's a meanie," I finished. "I think his black hair grease is seeping into his brain and heart."

She giggled. "He used to be the town dentist, but jabbed people too hard in the mouth, so nobody went to him anymore. Old teacher left town, so Mr. Dobbins was offered the post, him being educated and all. He hates the fact that he has to be a teacher now."

"I'm not overly fond of him being a teacher either."

We sat chewing, me on cheese and tomato slices and her on cold ham, cornbread, and hardboiled eggs. I was trying to raise the subject of whether she'd like to come over to my house for a visit, but was afraid I'd say something that would make her not want to be my friend.

"My cat just had kits. Five of them." Amy wiped her mouth with a napkin, reminding me to pull mine out.

I searched my brain for something equally impressive. "Miss Ada says we need more hens, so she's letting the chicken have chicks."

"Oh my, I love a chick. Until they poop on you, that is," Amy said, giggling.

To my surprise, a giggle slipped out of me, too. "You can

come over and meet them when they hatch, if you want."

She clapped twice, smiled, and took a bite of egg. "I would love to," she said, spraying me with a few egg flicks. "I haven't been invited to anyone's house for—" She stopped talking and her face fell, like she'd said something wrong. She studied her hands, then peeked at me with big, blinking eyes.

"Good, that's settled," I told her, and dug through my satchel until I found a molasses cookie. Breaking it, I grandly handed Amy the bigger half. "Here you go. Amy Lawrence, I think that you and I were meant to be friends."

Looking up, she gave me a shy grin. "And I think St. Petersburg just got a whole lot more tolerable." She let out a small hiccup and pointed. "I declare, I think Sid Sawyer and Joe Harper are coming this way."

The sight of Sid and his shaggy-headed friend walking along the streambed made me remember the witchy bet. The next question I wanted to ask Amy might break our delicate thread of friendship, but I needed to know. "Amy, do you reckon we're too old to be having adventures?"

Amy's glower and shaking head were a beautiful thing to behold. "No! My daddy leaves me alone most nights. I'd be having adventures all the time if I had someone to have 'em with."

My sigh of blessed relief left me nearly breathless. I could only smile.

"But sometimes I need to stay home and take care of him," she said. "He just gets sad and then gets sick from too much drink, but it's all on account of my mama dying. He's a good daddy."

I nodded, looking down at the streambed. Joe and Sid seemed to be arguing about something or other. I didn't feel like telling about Mama's sadness. Whiskey for men was one thing, but a mama who ignored you was quite another. "If your daddy gets in trouble, I'll tell my daddy to go easy."

Amy's eyes got shiny. "Would you?" She had a happy, trembly look about her and held out a pinky finger. "Becky Thatcher, I know we practically just met and all, but will you be my best friend?"

Putting out my own pinky finger, I smiled so big it hurt. It's nice that those kind of things transferred with different towns, because I knew just what to do. Shaking pinkies wasn't nearly as dramatic as my blood pact with Bill Chaney back in Riley, but girl friendship pacts were more likeable in a way. We linked fingers.

"Amy Lawrence," I said, "I vow my eternal loyalty to our friendship and will never abandon you for the likes of anyone. I also promise to make a sworn enemy of anyone talking badly about you or your daddy."

She smiled back. "That was awful nice. Becky Thatcher, I will . . ." She frowned.

"Vow eternal loyalty—"

"Yes! I will vow eternal loyalty to our friendship and make an enemy of anyone who doesn't like you."

"A *sworn* enemy," I reminded her.

"A *sworn* enemy," she repeated.

We shook and wiped lunch crumbs off our laps just as Sid Sawyer joined us. Joe stayed at the stream, throwing sticks at the water.

"Hello, Becky. Amy."

Amy gave a little wave. "Hello, Sid."

"Look here." He held out a few torn papers no bigger than a playing card and what looked like ragged bits of dried grass. "Found it behind the schoolhouse. Pile of burned matches, too."

"Tobacco!" My declaration caused a few heads to whip around.

"Shh! Somebody's been smoking behind there."

"I didn't know Mr. Dobbins smoked," Amy said. "He used to be a dentist so he should know better." She wrinkled her nose. "His teeth ain't the best, anyhow."

"That one tooth of his looks like a rotten raisin," I agreed. "Probably from eating all his students' sweets."

Sid waved a hand at our talk. "No, he don't smoke. My money's on Davy Fry." He pointed to a boy tossing rocks at a bird's nest on the other side of the stream. "Say, we're all trying for Witchy Widow Douglas's pot the Saturday after this one. Thought you might want to know."

You thought right. "How come you're not doing the stealing this Saturday?"

"There's a full moon that night and her powers are sure to be too strong for us." He had an excited twinkle in his eye, just like Jon did when he talked about items of a superstitious nature. "Reckon you all might want to hold our bet money for us when the time comes?"

Hmph. "I reckon me and Amy will be doing that bet right along with you." I searched Amy's face for permission. She *had* said she was up for some adventure.

Her eyes widened, but she put on a determined expression. "We sure will."

Sid frowned. "Joe barely agreed to you all holding the money. There's no way he'll let girls in."

"Money's money," I said. "We'd fatten up the winnings pot. How much to get in?"

Sid looked up through the cottonwoods, considering. Finally he shrugged. "Gotta put in thirty cents. And I gotta talk to Joe about it and make sure he agrees."

"Fine," I told him. "You'll have your thirty cents, and come that Saturday night, Amy and I will have the whole pot."

"We'll see about that," he said, rubbing his hands together. "I know a few tricks to help me around a witch and her witch hound."

"As it so happens," I called to him as he walked off, "so do I."

Amy Lawrence poked me gently on the elbow. "You do?" She sucked on her lower lip and stared at me with worried eyes.

I patted her knee. "I do. Don't you worry, Amy. A full moon may not be good for stealing from witches, but it's perfect for getting protective dirt."

She tilted her head sideways and cleared her throat. "Getting protective dirt from where?"

I could see she was in danger of backing out and I didn't want to overwhelm her with details that included the word "graveyard." I also suspected that sharing the news about the loose and murderous Pritchards would be unwise. "We'll talk about it later," I told her.

I'd never actually attempted using cemetery dirt to ward off a witch, but I'd spent enough time listening to Jon's stories to pick up that trick and others. Jon knew more about superstitious business than anybody I could think of. And while Daddy would probably put any sort of witchy dealings in the category of *irresponsible* and *not grown-up*, Jon would have eaten this adventure up like a hunk of lemon pie.

I sure wished he was with me to help.

No, I just wished he was with me.

Chapter Four

<hr>

Beetles and Pritchards and witches
(and Sam Clemens, to boot)

Early morning was the best time to dig up gull beetles, the ugly kind with feelers that could scare the hair off a baby. I didn't know why they were called gull beetles, but I reckoned it had something to do with the high-pitched shriek Ruth Bumpner would let out when she found one buried in her egg salad sometime in the next week or so.

I'd been around most of the backyard by six o'clock Saturday morning, lifting the big stones that bordered our garden. At six thirty I headed around front and bent over the roots of our big oak, as the stinkiest stinkbugs tended to gnaw on cool, woody dirt. Across the road and down the street, I saw that the writer man, Sam Clemens, was rocking again. This time his steaming cup was forgotten while he jotted something down and chuckled to himself. I wondered what sort of knee-slapper he was thinking up and whether Sid and Tom would get to hear it.

There's a thought. Maybe Mr. Sam Clemens would have some inside information about the Sawyer boys that could help me with the witchy bet and with getting a little revenge on Tattletale Tom.

But before I could walk over and pick his brain, Miss Ada shouted at me to come in for breakfast. I ran upstairs real quick to wash up and change clothes. Mama's door was open. She was standing by her bed, folding clothes.

"Hey, Mama," I said. "Miss Ada says breakfast is ready if you want to eat with me and Daddy."

She lifted her chin to look at me. The shadows on her face were deep this morning, like the dark sadness she carried around had risen from her heart and settled under her eyes. She looked awful weary. Too weary to bother with me.

"Not today," she said. When she spoke, Mama's voice was quiet and fragile and broken sounding. Like a bee's wing being torn. She returned to folding, placing another shirt onto a small stack. They were boys' shirts, several of them still holding stains that I remember her chiding Jon for making.

Blinking my eyes in the dusty hallway, I slapped at my front on the way downstairs, trying to loosen the pressing-down feeling that had settled onto my chest. I poked my head in the kitchen and saw that Miss Ada was stirring something. Grits, maybe.

"Becky, join me in the dining room," Daddy's voice boomed through the hallway. "And bring me some of whatever Ada's got on the stove."

I brought us each a bowl of cheesy grits and sat down across from him. It was strange eating outside of the kitchen. It felt wrong somehow, like there was too much extra space and not enough people to fill it.

Daddy's eyes were raw and red. "What are you dressed so nicely for?" he asked. "It's Saturday."

I had stuffed myself into another fishskin and was determined to be extra good, so that Daddy wouldn't have any reason to think his daughter would be sneaking out to rob grave dirt that evening. "My new friend Amy's coming over. We're going to look around town and see if any chicks have hatched and maybe bake something." *And then talk over how to use protective dirt against a witch and her witch hound.* "What are you doing?"

He blew on a spoonful, let it rest for a second, then blew again. When the grits hit his mouth, Daddy let out a soft sigh, like maybe he should permanently reconsider his coffee-only breakfasts. "I have a meeting at the courthouse. The Pritchards have struck in the town of Shirley, just north of us." He scooped up a few more mouthfuls.

I took a big bite and sighed happily like Daddy had done. *Mmm.* Miss Ada put in extra cheese, I could tell. "Any chance they'll come here? I saw that poster in your office." I continued shoveling in my grits. Marauder talk made me hungry.

"They must have a considerable load of stolen items and cash money at this point, so we know they'll be stashing it somewhere, but it's not likely they'll come to St. Petersburg with the Law on their tails. There's not enough places for them to cause trouble in this town. I don't believe the sheriff here has ever dealt with much more than a few dog bites."

I picked at my knee scab, scratching the itchy parts and

trying to peel off the hardened edges. "You okay, Daddy? You never eat breakfast."

"Well, I needed something in my belly this morning." He rubbed his substantial paunch. "Your mama had a rough night and I didn't get any sleep. I made the mistake of trying to talk to her." He sighed. "She just needs some alone time."

I pushed my bowl to the center of the table. "She seems to have plenty." I drummed my fingers to keep from saying that people who need to be alone all the time oughtn't get married and have children in the first place.

"Shh, Becky. It's hardest on a mother. They need the most time to let go." Pushing his breakfast aside, he placed his plate-size hands over mine. "I'm glad Amy's coming over." A tired smile spread over his cheeks. "Shows me you're growing up and finding interests other than sneaking out of the house."

I covered up a snort with a fake cough. I didn't want to grow up, and I'd be sneaking out of the house that very night.

"You all right?"

I nodded, pulled my bowl toward me, and kept eating. The last scrape of grits was lumpy, and I had a hard time getting it down my throat. While I swallowed extra hard, I stared at the two empty places at the table and wondered whether Mama had chosen to let me go instead of Jon.

A hesitant knock at the front door saved me from getting wound up and sharing any of that business with Daddy.

"Come in!" I shouted real loud, ignoring Daddy's *a more grown up young lady wouldn't shout like that* wince. "Amy's here. She and I are gonna take a lunch and eat by the river today, Daddy."

"Fine, fine," he said, returning to his bowl of grits.

"Just wait for me in the kitchen, Amy!" I ran upstairs for Jon's old schoolbag, which I'd turned into my adventuring satchel, and made sure his marbles were inside. I felt a powerful temptation to slip outta my fishskin and into overalls, but I didn't.

My fist hung in the air for a good minute before I knocked on Mama's door on the way back downstairs. "Mama? Amy Lawrence and me are going to town. You need anything?" I knew she didn't, but some part of me was dying to hear her voice again.

A few hesitant footsteps creaked along her floor. She came close enough to the closed door for part of her shadow to poke out.

"Mama? You need anything?" I waited, but she didn't say a word. Kneeling real quiet, I touched Mama's shadow until it silently withdrew from under the door. Then I stood and stomped downstairs.

Right before we left, Miss Ada gave me a lunch and a bag full of cherries and asked if we'd fetch her a five-pound sack of sugar while we were out. We scooted out the back door into a perfect September day, nice and sunny with a wispy breeze. There were only a few white clouds bundled together in the otherwise blue sky, and they were too high and far away to give a thought to.

"I'll teach you how to send the pits flying, if you want," I told Amy, hefting the bag of cherries.

"Oh, that'd be awful nice," she said. "I've never tried."

"We'll get that changed," I promised. "You'll be spitting like a mad cat soon enough."

As we passed the Sawyer house, I saw Tom and Sid in their side garden. Tom was yanking beans and putting them into a basket. Sid was plucking overripe tomatoes and eyeing Tom's rear end like it was a mighty tempting target.

"How did their mama die?" I asked. It was a might early to ask Amy about her own mama, but the Sawyers' mama was safe asking territory.

"I think it was a fever of some kind, but I couldn't say for certain. They lived across the river, but got sent here after she died. Word is, Tom squallered plenty, screaming and throwing his dirty nappies around and causing trouble. Drove his daddy crazy enough to dump both Sid and Tom with Aunt Polly. Tom's been making up for it by being a goody-goody ever since." Amy half-grinned at me, looking for agreement.

"Sure he has," I said. "He'd probably lick Aunt Polly's silver to a shine if she'd let him." I was glad to be well out of nappies when Jon died or I might have done some throwing myself. With Mama ignoring me the way she was, that would have made for a stinky house.

Amy grabbed my hand and squeezed hard. "Now, tell me your big plans for this witchy bet with the Widow Douglas."

I gave her the details. She tugged her lower lip into her mouth, looking bucktoothed by the time I finished.

"I've never stolen a thing in my life, and a witch is bound to be watching all the time. Look!" Amy let out a little cry and jammed her finger into my side. "There she is now!"

Sure enough, one block over from us the Widow Douglas was walking along the road toward her house, the big blue tick-hound by her side. She carried a mug that let off a line of white steam. Just as she passed a small yellow house with a strip of wilted mums bordering its front fence, the Widow gave a little glance to her right and left and dumped the contents of the cup right on the flowers.

"See there." Amy pointed. "That's Ruth Bumpner's house. She just poured something witchy right in the garden!"

"Whatever was in that cup was cursed for sure," I agreed. "But Ruth Bumpner is as mean as Mr. Dobbins, and I suspect her mama's not much better, so I can't say I'm opposed."

"She's watching us now!"

The Widow had reached her own yard. She peered our way over a set of little glasses. Her gray hair was hanging down, roped around her shoulder in a long braid, not tucked up in a tight bun like most old ladies. The hound padded back and forth across the yard, thick strands of drool running down its jowls.

"That dog has teeth over an inch long," Amy whispered, as though the Widow was much closer. "Last year he killed and dragged a young black bear onto the lawn. The Widow left it there for a week to rot."

I gulped. "We'll be fine. Bears aren't all that fast. You're a pretty good runner, right?" Ignoring her horrified face, I gathered my courage and gave the Widow a friendly wave to show that I wasn't gossiping about her this time. Amy took in a loud breath.

"Amy, you can't go gasping like that," I hissed at her. "You gotta learn to control your noises." I made a note to tell her not to speak on the night we went stealing. Not that it would really count as *stealing* when a witch was involved.

"Why'd you wave at her? She just looks mad, Becky. She's witching us right now." Amy poked my side and let out a little squeak. "See her mouth moving?"

I did. Part of me suspected the Widow was just talking to her dog, whose head was lolling back and forth underneath her fingers, but Amy was most likely right. We were being witched. I grabbed my best friend's elbow and pushed her down the road, and was lucky enough to find us two rocks on the ground. I handed one to her. "Amy, listen to me. Squeeze this rock tight and say these words:

> *Witchy spell, witchy spell, bother me none,*
> *Shave down a horse, and bite off the sun,*
> *Horny toad, pig slop, kitten in a barn,*
> *Your witchy spell don't bother me a darn."*

Amy looked pale, but repeated the words with my help. "Now what?"

"Throw that rock as far as you can, Amy. That'll take the spell off us." I hauled back and threw my rock down the road.

Amy did the same and flinched when hers landed right outside of the Bumpner house.

"Good," I said. "Maybe Pinchy-face will pick up your rock and get cursed."

Gripping my dress sleeve, Amy shook me a little. "What? Cursed?"

I shrugged. "Better her than us. Just a little curse, probably. A wart maybe."

Amy released my sleeve, her mouth twisting toward one ear.

"Becky, are you awful sure we should do this bet?"

I fixed her with a stern gaze. "Amy Lawrence, I have two questions for you. Do you trust me as a best friend, and do you trust that I would never, *ever* allow harm to come to you?"

She looked properly ashamed and took two big breaths. "Of course. I told you I was ready to have adventures."

"Good." I took her hand in mine and turned us around. "Then let's go settle this bet business right now. We'll talk to Sid and make sure we're good and in." I smiled to remind her that everything would be just fine. "Just think of that five dollars, Amy. Why, we could buy anything in the world with that! We could buy a ticket on a steamboat and go all the way to the ocean maybe. Besides," I said, putting my arm around her back, "all we need is some dirt from a graveyard under the moonlight, taken from a bad man's grave, and the Widow Witch can't touch us."

Amy shrugged my arm off and stopped walking. She turned to face me. "Becky Thatcher, is that the honest truth?"

I scratched an itch. St. Petersburg sure was full of skitters. "Sure it is. Follow me."

When the Sawyer porch came back into view, it wasn't Sid we saw, but Tom. He was rocking in a chair next to Sam Clemens and the two of them looked to be having a bully of a chat.

"He's probably telling about every bad thing Sid's ever done," I said.

Amy laughed. "I reckon there's a piece or two about you, too, Becky. He found out it was you who hit him with that spitball. Ruth Bumpner told at school yesterday."

That Pinchy-face has a prank coming her way. "He deserved it for laughing at you. Let's go see what he's blabbing about." When we stepped onto the porch, both Tom and Sam stopped their jabbering and Tom turned red as a ripe apple, which told me exactly who he'd been snitching on. "Where's Sid?" I asked.

"Somewhere with Joe Harper," Tom said, frowny-pouting while he looked down the road. "They wouldn't let me along."

Amy coughed politely to cover her laugh, but I just fixed him with a glare. "Tom Sawyer, if you're looking for someone to feel sorry for you, you best go look in a mirror. Nobody else is gonna do it."

"You must be Becky Thatcher," Sam Clemens said, recognition lighting up his eyes when he looked at my black braids. "I don't believe we were properly introduced last time we met. Tom's just been telling me about you."

Tom blushed even harder and I opened my mouth to give him a verbal licking.

"And this must be Amy Lawrence," Sam said quickly, smiling at Amy. "Tom tells me you and Becky are fast friends. Say, you got something to write with?" One of Sam's hands went to his head and knocked against it. The other held up a broken pencil. "I have to get this sentence out of my brain before it flies away."

I gave him a good stare. "A sentence flying away?"

"Sure. Haven't you ever wanted to say something to somebody, but when you get right there in front of them, you find your words went and hid somewhere?"

That happened near every time I'd tried to talk to Mama during the last year. I dug in my adventuring satchel for a pencil, jumped at a skitter bite, and out came my bag of marbles. The leather tie must've been loose, because they spilled all over the porch. "Dumb skitter," I explained, bending to gather the marbles. "Don't you touch those," I warned Tom, who had bent over to help.

"The skitters are hanging on late this year," Sam agreed while Amy and I scooted around the porch, plucking up marbles. "We need a frost to blast them all dead." He bent to pick a marble up and I let him. "These don't look like shooters. They look mighty special."

"Sure do," said Amy, who hadn't seen them before.

They were right about the marbles being special. I hardly ever took them out all at once, but to see them that way was a wonder. Some had shapes and figures painted on them, tiny and real-looking. Trees and fishes and frogs and watermelons. One looked like a crystal ball. Others were pretty just for the sake that they were Jon's. Sam helped me pick up the rest and we dropped them back in the sack. "Where'd you get these?"

I tied the leather strap tight and tucked the marbles away. "Belonged to my brother."

"Oh? Where's he been?" Sam asked. "Haven't seen him around."

"He died," Tom said, then clapped a hand over his mouth. "At least that's what I heard," he mumbled, studying the porch floor.

I hated the thought of Tom Sawyer talking about my Jon, but I didn't figure that particular instance counted as tattling. "Been dead about a year now, sir," I told Sam.

His eyes got cloudy. "I'm sorry. I had two brothers and a

sister die when I was young. And my brother Henry died two years ago on the river." His lips formed a straight line, turning in on themselves and pressing hard. The pencil I gave him looked fit to break in the grip he was giving it.

I shifted my weight back and forth. Half of me wanted to leave. The other half wanted Amy and Tom to disappear so I could ask Sam if his mama had given up on life after her children died, and if she had given up on Sam along with it. "I'm real sorry for you, too."

"So am I," Amy Lawrence said.

"Me too," Tom echoed. He eyed me nervously and wiggled like he was about to wet his pants. "Say, I got something to tell," he said, a hopeful look lighting up his pasty face.

"I declare, Amy Lawrence, it's an awful nice day," I said, ignoring Tom. "I haven't seen such a day for weeks. Makes a body want to find Sid Sawyer and go fishing, don't it?"

"It's about trouble," Tom went on.

If Tom Sawyer figured I'd be interested in trouble, that was the same as him saying me and mishaps got along like bees and honey. Well, I'd be showing *his* tattling behind some trouble as soon as I got around to it. But seeing as I was in the company of a riverboat pilot, I stayed polite and just narrowed my eyes a little. "So?"

"Aunt Polly heard that some boys broke into the dry-goods store and stole candy and all the Reed's tobacco they got," Tom continued. "They guess it was boys, anyway. Who else would steal candy and tobacco?" He grinned at me.

"I might," I said, just to shock the smile off his face. Worked, too.

His lips fell like someone who'd opened up a present and found a pile of cat poop. "I better get back inside. Aunt Polly wanted some help with . . ." He trailed off, looking miserable, kicked at an imaginary rock on the porch, and shuffled into the house.

"Good riddance," I said under my breath.

"Mr. Clemens," Amy said, "Becky told me you're waiting on a part to come in. Is your steamboat gonna be in town much longer?"

"Another week at least. I don't mind, though. I like this town." He stared off the porch, taking in the view from the Sawyer place. "Here comes Sid."

Far down the road, not more than an inch-high blob in the distance, I saw the easy sway of Sid Sawyer's arms. I imagined he was whistling. How two brothers can be different as cookies and collards is beyond me. I grinned at Sam. "Well, you better write that thought down before it runs away."

"*Flies* away. A single word can make a world of difference."

What that was supposed to mean, I didn't rightly know or care. "Right, sir. You go ahead and keep that pencil. Come on, Amy." I reached for her hand.

We were halfway down the steps when he called to me. "Becky Thatcher?"

"Yes, sir?"

"I been hearing some talk about a certain boys' bet, and I understand you're taking part?" He jerked his head toward the Widow Douglas's house.

Ooo, that Tom Sawyer must have opened his fat mouth. I slapped an innocent look on my face. "I don't know what on earth you're talking about."

"She leaves her back windows unlocked and open. She likes the night air come autumn."

Well, well. An open window was just the kind of thing that's good to know for a stealing adventure. "How would you know, sir? Not that I care. Just curious."

"I've had opportunity to talk with her a time or two, when she's out gardening. Besides, I don't mind talking to a witch." He winked again.

Amy nudged me so hard in the ribs that I nearly gave her a shove back.

Did that wink mean he knew she *was* a witch, or that he thought for certain that she *wasn't* a witch? Hard to say. I hated when adults spoke in riddles that only they knew the answers to. Plain rude, that's what it was.

I cleared my throat. "So the Widow *is* a witch? That's the truth?" When he didn't speak, I pressed him with the Bible quote from Mrs. Sprague. Adults can't resist a good Bible quote. "The truth will set you free, you know. John from the Bible said that."

"That a fact?" Sam chuckled. "Well, the truth about the Widow Douglas is something you'd best figure out on your own."

Amy made a whimpering noise beside me, like she didn't want to figure much of anything out when it came to the Widow.

"All right, sir. We best get going." I looked down the road, but Sid had disappeared. Darn it. We were down the last step, when Sam spoke again. "One more thing, girls."

"Yes, sir?"

"Charlie likes bacon."

"Who's Charlie?" asked Amy.

"The Widow's hound dog. Really it's Charlemagne, but she calls him Charlie. That dog just loves a piece of bacon."

I let out a snort. "I'll bet that dog probably likes a whole pig even better."

"Probably," Sam acknowledged. "He's a hunting dog, that's for certain." And with that, Sam Clemens tipped his hat at us and started scribbling his sentence.

Chapter Five

———◆———

Scabs and strategy

I led us around the Sawyer house until we reached a nice patch of trees at the corner of the block. It was as good a place as any for a spitting lesson. I worried the fruit flesh off a cherry with my tongue, looked around to make sure Aunt Polly wasn't in sight, then leaned back and spit the pit a good fifteen feet. It sailed right into their backyard.

Amy tried to spit too. She didn't get but three feet, so I shared my opinions with her on the best way to go about it. We sat down and were halfway through the bag when a tap on my shoulder had me swallowing a pit. I coughed it into my hand and looked up at Sid Sawyer. "Where'd you come from?"

Sid laughed. "Made plans to meet Joe around here, but I didn't want Tom following us, so I left and doubled back. I see you ladies are having a spitting contest. Mind if join you? I don't even need a cherry." He bowed gallantly and let loose with the biggest wad of phlegm I've seen in three states. It went clear over the fence.

I gave him a nod of approval. Then I chewed another cherry and sent my pit a foot farther.

"Pretty good," he said. "Hey! Watch this." He turned a neat cartwheel.

"I can do two in a row, but not in this," I said, pulling on my dress.

Joe Harper rounded the corner humming to himself. He made his way over to where we three stood and slapped Sid on the back. With a sly glance at Amy and me, he chuckled and rubbed his hands together. "I've decided that since you have no chance of stealing from the Widow Witch, the Christian thing to do is to let you give it a try. Besides, extra losers means extra jingle in my pocket when Sid and I win. You ladies ready to pay up?"

"Just getting around to it." I dug into my satchel for the coins.

Joe snatched the money from my hand and began counting. He squinched up his eyes and counted out loud. Then he glared at me. "You're cheating us."

"What do you mean? It's all there."

He counted again and thrust a finger in my face. "It's thirty cents *per person*." He smiled real mean. "Pay up or she's outta the bet," he snapped at me, jerking his head toward Amy.

"Sid said we just had to pay thirty cents," I argued back.

"If you're both gonna be doing the stealing, then you both have to pay right now or you're out. Didn't want no girls doing it anyway. Y'all don't have the grit for this kinda thing." His lips curved up in a wicked smile. "But we'll take this thirty cents as a payment toward whatever bet we do next. How's that sound?"

"Sounds like this." I shot him my best evil eye and spit near his feet. It was bad form to make us pay now or never and even worse form to keep the money we'd already paid. I looked at Amy, but she shook her head. She didn't have five cents, let alone thirty. I was disappointed to see that she seemed to be relieved. *Think,* Becky. *Think, think, think.*

"Will you trade for it?" I asked.

Joe hesitated. "Got anything good? Skipping rocks or an arrowhead? Lost my best arrowhead to Davy Fry last week."

"Not on me. And arrowheads are worth way more than thirty cents," I added, which was a lie, but Jon always said to establish a high value on trading goods.

"Trade something else, then," Joe demanded. "Whatcha got?"

I thought for a minute about my various treasures, then reached into my satchel. Inside an empty box of playing cards was a prize that might do the trick. I opened the box and tilted out a square of folded cloth. Unfolding the fabric, I presented him with the contents. "Got this daddy longlegs spider. Only had three legs to start with. Probably has powers of some sort."

"That?" Joe leaned close and sniffed the spider. "It's dead! Why, you plucked off the other legs and made it die. I'm no fool."

I shrugged and offered him a spit cherry with my free hand. "Maybe I did and maybe I didn't. All I know is that the murderous Pritchard brothers might be dropping into town any day now, and it'd be foolish to turn down an item of such protective power." I shook my head to show what a shame it'd be.

"I told Sid what my daddy said about those outlaws. Figured he would've warned you about the likes of them." I frowned at the spider in my hand and folded the cloth back over it. "Come to think on it, maybe I don't want to trade this after all."

Amy managed to keep quiet despite her eyes nearly popping from their sockets to bop me on the head for keeping secrets from her. I hadn't gotten a chance to tell her about the Pritchards yet, or about the rules of acceptable exaggeration when making a trade. I widened my own eyes to the point of popping to tell her to keep hushed up and let me finish our business first and explain things later.

"Hold on." Joe took the cherry, popped it in his mouth, and snatched the daddy longlegs. After a brief examination, he put it in the bib of his overalls. "All right, that's worth five, but you got to give more'n a spider to make up the rest. That's twenty-five cents you owe."

Twenty-five cents would mean trading a mighty big item. Not even a dead mouse would get me that. I thought and thought, and my stomach turned once the answer came to me. Before I could chicken out, I lifted my dress just enough to show my knee, revealing the huge scab from the day outside of Mrs. Sprague's house. "I'll let you pick this."

Amy clutched my shoulder. "Becky, no!"

"Say, look at that!" Joe's fingers twitched and he bent down for a closer look. "That's a real nice one." He frowned. "You won't holler or nothing?"

I shook my head, trying to pretend Amy Lawrence hadn't just made a gagging noise. "But you can't do it now. You have to wait until after we do some chores for Miss Ada. I don't want to walk around town with a bloody leg." I also didn't want to go cemetery-dirt-grabbing with a sore knee, but as Jon used to say, some things in life are worth sacrificing. He usually said that about school, but I reckoned knees counted too.

"Fine. That'll do." He looked at Sid. "Did you tell 'em the rules?"

"Nope."

"Okay, look here. Rules are you got to do the stealing after eleven o'clock at night next Saturday. We'll meet at the schoolhouse for dumping and showing at one o'clock, so that's two hours for the stealing. If we happen to bump into each other at the Widow's, there'll be no pushing or shoving or shouting. And if we get caught, it's each man for himself." His cheeks got pinkish. "Or girl, I guess. You're for yourselves too. If somebody gets in a tight spot with the witch, we ain't gonna come save you. Got it?"

"Got it," I said, answering for me and Amy. "If you get in a tight spot, we'll just be saving ourselves, too. And if you die, we'll promise to tell your mama that you weren't stealing."

Joe looked a little sweaty at my promise. "Okay. We'll do the same." He punched Sid's shoulder. "Let's go fishing before that brother of yours tries to follow us." He pointed to the porch, where Tom was talking to Sam Clemens again.

Sid let out a real good belch. "Naw, he won't follow us. He's too busy spilling our secrets to Sam Clemens. What kind of writer would want to hear dumb stories about St. Petersburg?"

Amy and I headed into town, where we walked smack into the Pritchard poster from Daddy's office. It had been copied and put up on the public notice board.

Amy pinched me lightly on the hip and got all quivery

lipped. "Oh, Becky, why didn't you tell me about them? You told Sid before me? I thought we were best friends."

The betrayal tore me up good before I realized why I'd told Sid first. "I told him on the way to school, first day I came. You and me hadn't even met yet, let alone made our pact. I was gonna tell real soon, swear to Heaven, I was."

She matched my sigh of relief. "That's all right, then. But shouldn't we be awful worried about the Pritchards? Especially with you giving away that three-legged spider?"

Well, the honest truth was that I'd lied just a little about that spider having powers, but stretching the facts to make a trade go your way was a lesson for another day. "Don't you worry, Amy. This town's too boring to ever have marauders get close enough to do anything interesting."

We stopped at Marley's Dry Goods Emporium for a sack of sugar, then crossed to the riverside and whipped through bushes, playing explorer until we found a nice spot by the water to eat lunch.

Amy let out a heavy breath. "We'll be okay tonight, won't we?"

I nodded and passed her a baking powder biscuit with strawberry preserves. "Just remember what I said about dipping your toes in sugar before you put your shoes on. Jon always said to sweeten your feet before getting into night mischief. You got sugar?" I sorted the rest of the food, laying it on one of Jon's handkerchiefs. Apples, cold ham, two slices of lemon ice-box cake, and a few more plain biscuits.

She licked red preserves from her fingers. "Yes. Sure you can sneak out again so soon after your daddy caught you?" she asked me, squirming a little. "We could always do it the Friday before the bet."

"Nope. It's best to have the dirt sit awhile to get real strong. And tonight's a full moon, which'll make the protection even more powerful. I'll come to your place around eleven thirty and do a little cat meow." I demonstrated. "Like that, only three of them. Then you do it back and we'll know we're both each other, and not something else."

"It's gotta be midnight when we get the dirt?"

I nodded, pulling apart two plain biscuits and sticking ham inside. "Jon got his information from all sorts of trusted folks who knew about spirits and such. The only thing that'll weaken a witch is midnight dirt from a bad man's grave under the moonlight. You know of any bad men who're dead in the cemetery here?" I handed her a ham biscuit.

"Thanks." Her features scrunched together in thought. "I haven't been to that cemetery much. Mama's on the other side of the river with her folks. They have a family plot and Daddy said it's what she would've wanted." She sighed. "He won't take us across to visit much."

"We'll make a raft just for visits," I promised her.

"Oh, Becky, will we? That sounds awful nice. Let's see, a bad man . . . Mama used to say that Old Robert Willis had about as many morals as a backwards-born mule."

"What's that mean?"

"Don't know what it means." She clucked her tongue a few times. "But Daddy once told me that Mr. Willis was the youngest of ten kids and never got anything to play with but dirt and chicken heads and that's why he was always swiping silly things, even as a grown man. Couldn't stay away from box puzzles and pop guns, but was too embarrassed to buy them."

The topic of store stealing made me think of the break-in at Marley's that Tom had mentioned, and how maybe it wasn't a boy who'd broken in. "Mr. Robert Willis sounds like our man," I told Amy.

She frowned. "Mrs. Willis knew about the stealing and always paid up, though."

"He didn't know she paid?"

"No, no."

"Then his grave dirt will be just fine." I searched my head for another way to help us out, since our chosen bad man's badness wasn't overly bad. "You don't know where a dead cat is, do you?"

Her mouth dropped open, loosening a stuck crumb on the side of her mouth. "How'd you know? One of the kittens is awful sick. Keeps getting shoved away from the teat. Becky Thatcher, what are you thinking?"

Across the river, a ruckus was happening between two fishermen on a log raft. I gave my ear four tugs to keep the sick-kitten information inside my head. "Nothing for now. But a dead cat comes in mighty handy for keeping away spirits. I'd like to have one for the cemetery, but we'll need it for sure at the Widow's house, as she'll have spirits around her. Maybe your kitten'll die by the time we go to the Widow Witch's?"

"Becky, you sound like you hope that kitten dies!"

I let my eyes follow a rowboat crossing to the Illinois side of the Mississippi. One place on the river the rower was in Missouri, and the next he was a whole state over. I wondered if he could feel the moment when he was someplace different or if it felt the same and he had to remind himself of the change.

"Amy Lawrence, I didn't mean it like that. I would never say, 'Let's *kill* a kitten,' but if a deceased one is coming to be available, it would be foolish not to take advantage of its spirit-repelling powers. You won't be helping it along or anything." *Besides*, I thought, feeling ornery, *it's just a kitten. Not a brother or a mama.*

Amy nodded, her cheeks pink and eyes shiny with unshed tears for the sick kitten. "You're right, I guess."

"Good. Just keep an eye out or a dog might eat it. Think you can put that kitten in a bag and keep it, if it dies?"

"I . . . I reckon I could."

"Good." I clapped her on the shoulder. "We'll do just fine at the cemetery tonight, and then we'll win that bet, and then I'll buy you a dress with my share of the winnings."

Amy had torn her dress on a branch during our exploring, and she was about as good at sewing as I was. I told her to give the dress to Mrs. Sprague to fix, but she said she was too embarrassed ("explorer" not being a real Christian game for young girls to play) and didn't want to lie about how the fabric got torn.

That's a beautiful and dangerous thing to have in a best friend, one that's not inclined to lie. Daddy would probably plunk honesty in the category of being responsible and grown-up, but telling the plain truth didn't suit my lifestyle much. I'd been gradually convincing Amy that most lies were right nice, because you were telling people what they wanted to hear, and what could be wrong with making people happy?

She liked that reasoning, and made me repeat it a few times to get it fixed in her head.

We worked our way through the food, Amy telling me how the cemetery was up past the picnic grounds and the old cave near Carver Hill, behind the Widow's house a ways.

"Becky, you don't think we'll run into the Pritchard brothers, do you?" Amy asked.

Shaking my head, I hunted for a throwing stone. "Why would thieves and murderers hang around a graveyard? Nothing to steal and the people are already dead." Finding a beauty, I launched the rock a good thirty feet, where it made a nice plop in the river. "No, they won't come near there. But speaking about meanies and the picnic grounds, I got a little idea about Mr. Dobbins and the school picnic next month." I reached for a slice of lemon cake.

She lit up, lifting the other slice. "What's that?"

"It has a little to do with hair grease and a little to do with a stinkbug that I've been saving for Tom Sawyer . . ."

After lunch, I walked Amy to her house on the other side of town and headed back to Willow Street. I was nearly home, when, from the corner of my eye, I saw something jump off the Sawyer porch. Puffing breath and quick footsteps followed behind me. I turned and felt my stomach slip down to my toes.

"Hey!" Joe Harper caught up to me. "Where are you going? Mama clipped my nails, but I kept this one away from her, just for you." He held up a finger and smiled at my scab. "Time to pay up."

Chapter Six

———•———

An unexpectedly fearful happening
at the cemetery

At eleven fifteen that night, I snuck out the back door with an extra set of Jon's clothes flung over my shoulder, half an apple pie in my hands, and my marbles stuffed deep into my front overall pocket. I peered down the road, making good and sure that Tom Sawyer wasn't watching from his porch for someone to tattle on. Crossing town only took five minutes because I was feeling extra spirited under the light of the full moon.

I let out three meows when I got to the Lawrence place and didn't get a single response. Tried three more times, but Amy never meowed back, so I tossed a pebble at her bedroom window.

"I'm here," Amy whispered, sticking her head out. "Just making sure Daddy's good and asleep."

"Brought you half a pie," I whispered back. "Miss Ada made extra." Maybe it would cheer her daddy up. I heard that misery loves company, but I suspected it would get along with pie, too. Also, I figured Amy was an inexperienced mischief-maker, and it didn't hurt to balance the idea of bad-doing with a reward of something good-tasting. "Where do you want it?"

"Kitchen table's fine, door's open. I'll be right there."

By then I'd been inside the house enough to see that an eleven-year-old girl without a mama or a Miss Ada to help had a time cleaning up after a daddy who has friends over to play cards. There were piles of crumbs in the counter corners, a few old spills on the kitchen floor that hadn't quite been wiped away, and a heap of tools and paint buckets by the back door, as though somebody had considered fixing something at one point but never got around to it. Amy said they'd had to burn all her mama's clothing because of her sickness, and her daddy'd gone crazy with grief and burned most everything else that belonged to Mrs. Lawrence. There wasn't much sign that Amy's mama had ever existed.

I walked around the kitchen thinking maybe Mr. Lawrence never got a talk about how being grown-up means you have to be responsible and clean up crumby counters and not set fire to things just because you're sad. In fact, being in that house made me realize that Amy and I were justified in making a little mischief, since we both had parents who didn't have the energy to care about much at all, let alone us.

I hadn't seen much of Mr. Lawrence when I'd visited Amy, but I could smell his whiskey and sense his heartache. Mama had the same sorrow about her, and it made me wonder if she and Mr. Lawrence couldn't have a nice chat over coffee.

I ran my hands over the paint buckets and tools. Sadness was a heavy thing. I had it bad right when Jon died, and could barely walk down the stairs. The pressure on my back and heart and mind was something awful. But the marbles helped. And the promise we shared.

Footfalls sounded by the staircase and Amy appeared, holding a finger to her lips. "He's snoring pretty good, but we should be quiet. That pie looks good."

Amy changed into Jon's overalls quickly and we were soon tramping through the woods behind the school. Past the picnic grounds, past the town kissing oak, past the old cave and into another patch of woods that surrounded St. Petersburg Cemetery. We followed a small trail around the back.

A cold spell had come through that twilight, and the sky was filling with clouds. The mist that hung over the river must have drifted inland a good ways because fog floated between the tombstones. It was pretty darn dark, but every time the clouds moved, a peep of haunted moon gave us a little light to see by. Not enough, though, so I went ahead and lit the lantern we'd taken from Amy's place.

"It's a ghostly night," Amy whispered.

"It sure is," I whispered back. "You know, Amy, I bet that's not fog at all, but spirits."

"I don't believe I like spirits much," she said, her voice quavering. "Tell 'em to go away, can't you?"

I dug in my pocket and handed her a piece of cloth I'd borrowed from the rag pile. "Tuck that into your shirt front."

"What for?"

I tucked my rag in and tugged to make sure it'd stay. "In case of evil spirits. They'll take one look at us and skeedaddle, thinking we're about to eat something at a picnic. Nobody goes to a picnic at night, so the spirits'll think it's daytime and head back to their waiting spots."

Amy looked doubtful, but pushed the cloth under her shirt. "Really?"

My, but I hate a doubter. "Really." *It couldn't hurt, anyway.*

She twitched beside me, knocking my side with her shaky hands. "I don't know if I like this particular adventure, Becky. You sure we have to wait until midnight?" Her face was pale in the moonlight.

"We sure do," I said, giving her hand a squeeze. "Now, where's that Robert Willis buried?"

We moved from grave to grave, holding the light up against the stones and reading the names and dates of life and death underneath. I only saw a few where the number of years from birth to death was under twenty, and only one that was Jon's forever age of seventeen. For a second, I imagined it was him under our feet and felt a sudden chill. It was a powerful kind of shivery, standing there on top of dead men and women.

"What time is it?" Amy sounded worried and I didn't blame her. There weren't too many gravestones left, and we still hadn't found Mr. Willis.

I checked the pocket watch I'd taken from Daddy's office. "Old Reliable says we've still got ten minutes. I'll keep an eye on the time and—say! Here it is." I pointed to the stone next to us. "Looks like he died just last year."

ROBERT HOMER WILLIS

1807–1859

BELOVED FATHER AND HUSBAND

I tapped the epitaph. "Hmm. He doesn't sound so bad, here. You sure he did all that stealing while he had a family?"

"Oh, sure. Daddy talks foolishness now and again, but not Mama, and I remember her saying Robert Willis was nothing but an overgrown child, snatching things and lying about it."

On that note, part of me wondered if an eleven-year-old would be sneaking protective dirt from *my* grave someday, on account of all the mischief I'd gotten up to.

Amy seemed to have the same thought. "Becky, did you steal that watch from your daddy?"

I swallowed at something stuck in my throat. "Borrowed it."

"You reckon stealing from a widow will count against us going to Heaven and all?"

"I don't think so," I lied. Truthfully, stealing from widows had to be right up there with coveting your neighbor's new fishing pole. Probably worse. "She's a witch, so the stealing don't count." That sounded pretty good, but I wasn't positive that witchiness cancelled out widowhood. "Quick, tell me something she's done around town that's proved she's a witch."

"Well," Amy said slowly, "there's the rumor about the Widow's dog being open to her coming inside and possessing it. And she doesn't go to church, except on Easter and Christmas . . ."

My own Mama hadn't gone to church since we arrived in

town, though Amy wouldn't know that. She wasn't always there either, on account of her daddy being sick some Sunday mornings. *Hmm.* "Well, people got to have good reason for thinking she's a witch. She's probably doing something witchy right now."

Amy firmed up at the possibility. "I'm sure you're right."

"Of course I'm right," I said, gaining confidence in the idea. "She's probably boiling something and chanting a bunch of spells."

Amy nodded eagerly, then frowned. "Like the ones you know?"

"Amy Lawrence, those aren't spells!" I paused to think. "They're mostly about how to *keep away* evil, you know. Maybe some are about luck and getting things, but that don't count."

"Of course not! No, I know! I know."

But she sounded suspiciously like someone who didn't know, and I didn't like it. I set the lantern next to the headstone. "Now, Amy, what I really want to talk about is the job we're supposed to be doing. This dirt'll help with the witch, but if that dog is possessed by demonly spirits, we'll have to have something to hold him off, too. I'm thinking a big piece of bac—"

"Shh!" Amy'd gone pop-eyed. She grabbed the lantern and blew it out. With her head, she motioned to a patch of trees.

Sure enough, two lights bobbed in and out of the oak trees, disappearing and reappearing like a couple of fire-eyed devils winking at each other in the darkness. Removing her hand from my mouth, she grabbed my arm and pulled me behind the headstone of Robert Willis.

Peeking around the stone brought no comfort. "It's getting closer," I whispered.

"Is it evil spirits?" Amy shook beside me.

"Course not!" Part of me suspected it *was* evil spirits and we were about to be escorted somehow into the gates of Hell, but that's not the sort of thing you share with your best friend, especially when you've convinced her to come to a cemetery at midnight to gather a sack of a bad man's grave dirt.

The lights seemed to circle and zigzag until I realized they were following the same path we'd taken to get to the graveyard. I caught sight of a person-shaped silhouette against the trees before clouds covered the moon completely.

"Those're no spirits, those're people," I said real soft.

"Let's just *go. Let's get out of here.*"

Gripping Amy's arm, I pulled her close until her nose was scrunched against mine. "Think of that five dollars, Amy. If we don't get this dirt, then the Widow Witch'll get us for sure. We have to be smart about this. Now let's just hush up."

With that, we pressed ourselves closer to the headstone, our bodies hunched low and our heads still touching. Amy pinched me good when I scratched a skitter bite through my overall pants. My fingernails were making a rough scritching sound, so she was right to do that and I wasn't too mad at her. Daddy says that's how you know you're real close to someone. You can get mad at each other like anything and still love each other like crazy.

That's how he and Jon were, I guess. They were always going back and forth about how Jon should be more serious about school and be a lawyer or something. How he should grow up and take responsibility and quit all his nonsense. I hated hearing that yelling, but they managed to get along perfect by the next day. Boys are like that, and girls hold grudges like they were cradling their own babies. That's what Miss Ada says, anyway.

The clouds were rolling again and little hints of moonlight shone down on the graveyard.

"There's two of them," Amy whispered. "Two men."

I pinched her hard, and her hand flew over her mouth. There, we were pinching-even. No need for a grudge at all. "Quiet! We're supposed to be hushed up, so don't talk," I reminded her. "Say, what's that in their hands?"

They'd paused at the opposite end of the graveyard and were having a powwow by low lantern light. One was taller than the other by a good hand's length.

The taller one passed some object to the other man and then they began walking slowly through the rows, pausing to peer at the tombstones much like Amy and I had done.

"Psst! Amy, can you see what they're holding?"

She didn't say anything, so I poked her real light.

"*Ow!* You said not to talk, and now you're talking. How am I supposed to—"

A voice rose and the lantern swung our way.

"Down," I whispered. "Keep still."

Footsteps sounded a few rows away from where we crouched. I was too busy hiding my head to think about peeking and hoped Amy wouldn't look up either. *Don't move, don't move, don't move.*

After what seemed like hours, the men walked back to the far corner of the cemetery.

"This it?" asked a voice.

At least I think that's what it said. It was hard to hear all ducked down. Lifting my head real slowly and making sure to stay tucked behind the tombstone, I tapped Amy until she jerked up too. I raised my eyebrows at her, asking if she recognized the voice, but she just breathed in and out. Maybe she couldn't see my eyebrows. It was blacker than a cast-iron pot whenever the moon tucked itself behind the clouds.

"Get to digging then," said one of them, throwing something onto the ground.

The other man dug for what seemed like forever. A gentle rain began to fall. The sound of shovel hitting dirt and the tall man barking orders was enough to allow us a whisper or two.

"They're robbing that grave," Amy said.

I nodded, then remembered she couldn't barely see me. "Seems so. Just be quiet."

"Hurry up," the taller man growled. "That's it. No, just leave it in there and open 'er up."

I started to sweat, or maybe it was just the rain soaking me. We were in a graveyard with two men who I was starting to suspect were the notorious Pritchards. The world felt blacker than black for a minute and I was certain my heart was going to burst through my chest, just so it could run off and find a better hiding spot. Good God in Heaven, if they found us spying on them, we'd be dead for certain! They'd even have a grave ready-dug for us. Not knowing if Amy knew who it was, I vowed not to bring it up. It'd just frighten her.

"All right, get to work on those things," the same man ordered. "Get 'em out!"

Get what out? What were they stealing from a dead man?

There was a low groaning and the sound of exertion. After a time, I heard more talk from the tall one. The short man was too busy digging up grave dirt.

". . . can't do it now . . . business down in Trittsville . . . can't mess with that sort of thing on a full moon . . . back to get it done . . . your place or the cave next week."

Full moon? Why, those men were as superstitious as me. And what *cave?* There wasn't but one cave in our area big enough to bother with, and that was the one near the school picnic grounds.

"Do they look good? You're supposed to be the expert on . . ." The tall one seemed to be circling the smaller man, who was still waist deep in the grave. Lightning struck and I saw the silhouette of a long blade flash in the tall man's hand. "—so I'll just give you a little shaving to keep you loyal."

Grave robbing was one thing, but seeing someone get mutilated was another. I didn't care to see a man get his face sliced off. "Get ready to run, Amy."

"What?"

I fixed my courage, sucked in a giant breath, and let out a solid scream. "Murder! Murder in the graveyard!" Yanking Amy up, I pushed her away from the path the men had taken to get to the cemetery. I figured we'd plunge into the bush for cover, risking whatever scratches were necessary to stay alive.

Amy wasn't moving fast at all. Instead, she stumbled along between the gravestones, whimpering. I made a note to talk to her about not dawdling during emergency situations, if we made it through the night.

While Amy froze near a set of blackberry bushes, I turned

to see the men standing stock-still. Their heads went this way and that, and I thanked Jesus for the rain, because it more than likely confused my voice's direction. Jesus must hate murder as much as me.

Then, as if a spell had broken, both men hurried our way. I was certain that the taller man had his knife gripped in one hand. I was also certain that I'd seen his face before.

On a poster in Daddy's law office.

Keeping a firm grip on the back of Amy's overalls, I hurled my best friend to the ground and shoved her into the dirt beneath the bushes. I plunged myself right beside her.

Rain poured down, but not so loud that I couldn't hear an awful sound. Straining and shoving my ears back toward the graveyard as far as I dared, I heard it again. A growl. A not-so-human growl coming from somewhere between us and the Pritchards. I only hoped the moon stayed covered and that whatever was making that awful sound stayed far away.

When the Pritchards were halfway across the graveyard and heading our way, a great beast rose and lunged at the legs of the shorter one, taking a hefty bite of something, by the sound of the unmanly scream. I couldn't get a decent look at Forney Pritchard's face, but it was sure to be twisted in a good amount of agony.

"Gimme that shovel, I'll kill that dog," Billy Pritchard shouted, grabbing the tool from his brother.

The massive animal jumped toward Billy's chest. Deep-throated barking was followed by two screaming men, lightning flashes, and a low, mournful howl.

I lifted my head in time to see Billy rush into a bush not two feet away. He whipped his head around, scanning the area. Any minute he'd see us. I couldn't let Amy die here in the cemetery. Besides being my best friend in the world, who would take care of her daddy?

I swallowed my fear, along with a small amount of vomit that had worked its way up my throat. Waiting until Billy Pritchard moved his legs, and timing my whisper with the shuffling of bush leaves, I said what I suspected might be my last words.

"When he comes after me, *run home*." I put my hand over Amy's mouth to keep her from replying and placed a farewell kiss on the back of my hand.

Then I bolted straight back through the cemetery, screaming at the top of my lungs in my very best pirate voice, "You'll never take me alive!"

But I was so busy running from Billy Pritchard that I wasn't watching the headstones properly. Right before I cleared the back fence, my hip connected with solid rock and down I went, my freshly-picked knee hitting the ground first. Sore as a kicked horny toad, I lifted my head to see the gaping holes in Billy Pritchard's top row of teeth. He jerked me to my feet, then knocked me back to the dirt.

Bending over, he spit at my chest. His breath stunk like spoiled mushrooms, but it was the shiny knife at my throat that got my attention. His black eyes were so close to mine that I saw the reflection of my own terrified face.

He smiled, his face dripping with rain. "I never planned on taking you alive. I reckon I'll start with your ears. Then I'll—"

"Murder!" shrieked the sweetest voice in the world. "Oh, murder again!" It came from the other side of the cemetery and I prayed that Amy would stay far away from Forney Pritchard, dog-bitten as he might be. "Here comes, um, well, here comes the Law!"

Billy cursed and released me. "Fine," he muttered. "You know my face?" he asked me. He tore the evil-spirit-repelling cloth right outta my shirt and jabbed me with his knife point.

I managed to shake my head.

"Better not. What's your name?"

I didn't answer.

He looked me up and down, sniffing like a dog. "I'll find out. Can't be too many little girls in this town who'd be fool enough to be at a graveyard at midnight."

"I'm a runaway," I managed to whisper. "From downriver."

"Maybe, maybe not. But if I hear word that you told on me, I don't care where you're from. I'll find you and your family and I'll see to it that none of you have mouths to talk with." With a final kick to my side, he ran off, leaving me to close my eyes and sink back into the holy ground.

Amy's quivering figure fell on me. She grabbed my shoulders and shook hard. "Oh, Becky," she cried softly, struggling to keep her voice quiet. "Are you murdered?"

I wasn't murdered, but my head was taking quite a banging on the dirt. "I'm not," I told her, and the shakes turned into a fierce embrace. "Not a hair harmed," I said, forcing my voice to sound strong and sure. "He was about to leave anyway."

She pinched up and down my arm, making sure I was good and alive. "He didn't try to kill you?"

I sat up and rubbed Amy's thumping from my head. "Maybe just a little, but mostly he wanted to scare us. So we wouldn't follow them."

Her lower lip stuck out, the frown casting a shadow over her chin. "Why would we ever follow two grave robbers? We're eleven years old."

That was a pretty good point. I took my time heaving myself into a sitting position, checking for my marble bag while I thought up an explanation. "Well," I reasoned, "we were out here, same as them. They probably reckoned we were robbing a grave of our own and would come after their next target." I watched her expression shift as she chewed on that thought.

She nodded slowly. "Makes sense."

"Sure it does. Let's give them a couple more minutes to get away, then head home." We huddled underneath a bush and watched the headstones for stray spirits. Then we heard it again.

Another drawn-out howl.

"What's that?" Amy asked, scooting close. "*Don't look,*" she begged.

The rain had stopped its pitter-patter, and the moon seemed to think it was safe to come out from behind the clouds for good. Stars came out of hiding as well, glowing in the night sky like an angel's firefly collection, as Mama used to say. Pushing myself to a crouch, I did what Jon would've done.

I looked.

Around the corner of the nearest tombstone poked the head of the Widow Douglas's enormous dog. One of his front legs had an ugly slash across it and his teeth were clenched around a piece of cloth. He was breathing heavy, eyes darting back and forth.

I stood and walked closer. The cloth was soaked through with slobber, but I could just make out the plaid pattern from

Billy Pritchard's shirt. What stood out more, though, was the fact that someone had gone and put the teeth of a giant bear inside that hound's mouth. I wouldn't be telling Amy, but they looked to be a good deal longer than an inch and were just as sharp as Billy's knife.

"Becky don't! You said yourself, he's a demon dog!"

"A demon dog that maybe saved our hides," I pointed out, slowing my advance.

"Probably just so he can get us good and proper next Saturday," Amy guessed.

I paused. "Well, he's still hurting right now." But after seeing those teeth, any charitable thoughts of tending the dog's wound had flown to the back of my mind to cower behind more pressing business, so I was awful glad when Charlemagne lifted himself from the ground and limped back toward town, taking the wad of shirt with him.

Instead of following, I scooted fives graves over and three down, back to Mr. Willis. Old Reliable said it was twenty minutes past midnight. Taking an old flour sack from Jon's bib pocket, I dug up a layer of wet grass and scraped four handfuls of dirt into the sack, taking care to replace the chunk of grass I'd ripped out. Then I pointed a route through the woods and started walking, sure to keep an eye out for more unfriendly lights among the trees.

Amy put her hand on my shoulder as we made our way through the trees, nearly causing me to scream bloody murder.

"Did you get the dirt on time?" she asked.

"Yep. It's still the witching hour so we're all set for the bet next Saturday."

"Maybe we've had too much of a fright to do the bet at all. Becky," she said in a trembly voice, "were those men the Pritchard brothers?"

I'd seen Billy Pritchard's face clear as day and could pretty well guarantee who his sidekick had been, but there was no use scaring the bejeezus out of my best friend. My own bejeezus had been scared enough for the both of us. And even though I was shaken up, I figured those Pritchards were probably far too busy being lawless to bother with me again. Telling Amy about Billy's threat would just lead to trouble.

"Hard to say," I told Amy. "Even if it was, they've gone and robbed someone who can't care about it. I say we keep our mouths shut as tight as that burglarized dead man's."

Even in the dark, I could tell Amy was biting her lip, considering. "You don't think we should tell?"

We were nearly down Carver Hill. There wasn't a soul in sight as the trees began to thin, so I stopped and faced Amy. "No, I don't think we should tell." I knew enough about marauders to know three things: They like to cause trouble, they like to get away with it, and they like to get revenge on any fool who tattles on them. The fool's family, too. Already having a deceased brother and a barely-there mama, I couldn't afford any family members in danger. Seeing the fear in Amy's eyes, I added, "Besides, you heard them: They're headed downriver to Trittsville."

Grabbing the unlit lantern from my hand, Amy clutched it to her chest and sniffled. "I don't think I've ever been so scared in my whole life. All I kept thinking was that I'm too young to die, especially wearing overalls in a graveyard at midnight."

Jon was too young to die.

I felt a bothersome pressure building up behind my eyes. A single tear slid down my cheek so I slapped my face, telling any others to hold off.

"Don't hit yourself like that!" Amy looked appalled before recovering enough to pat my arm. "Now that's all right, you can cry."

"I don't feel like it now."

Her face squinched up, like she was thinking about doing some crying herself. "I cry about Mama sometimes. Lots of times, really. I'm scared Daddy won't ever get better without her." Her lips started twisting like they were avoiding a skitter or something.

I put a hand on her shoulder. "It's okay to cry," I whispered.

She shook her head something fierce. "Oh, slap me quick, Becky!"

So I reached out and gave her a nice firm slap. "There now. But you can still cry if you want."

She looked a little shocked that I'd gone ahead and smacked her, but seemed grateful, too. "Thanks, but I don't feel like it anymore either. Becky?"

"Yes?"

"Thank you for saving my life back there. I . . . I won't let you down next Saturday." Squeezing her shoulder, I placed my forehead against hers. "I know you won't. We'll have just about the biggest adventure of our lives and beat those boys to boot. And you saved my life right back, so don't get too mushy. Let's go home," I suggested. Leading the way, I hurried Amy past the dark houses of St. Petersburg, nerves adding a quickness to my steps that I couldn't hardly control.

We stood at her door in silence for a few minutes, then I ran home with hazy images of Pritchards and ghosts and Jon floating around every corner.

Chapter Seven

———◆———

A most disturbing threat and a lesson in storytelling

An awful nightmare about the Pritchards and graves and caves had kept me company throughout the night, and when I woke up all twisted in my sheets on Monday morning, a skitter was taking a bath in my rubbed-open scab. Thanks to my scuffling about, any healing my knee had done on Sunday was ruined. Jon would've loved the sight of it. Grumbling at the thought of another day spent with Mr. Dobbins, I slipped on clothes and yanked the tangles from my hair. My grumbling increased when I realized that the kitchen smelled like nothing, which meant there'd be a pot of plain oatmeal waiting for me.

Yanking at my dark blue fishskin during breakfast, I said a silent curse to whichever fool had thought up starch. The dress itched like the devil. Before I made it out the door, Miss Ada told me no less than three times to quit scratching at my arms and belly. I made sure to take fishing line, a sewing needle, dry beans, and a Bible for me and Amy. I figured we'd make us a little extra witch protection during the lunch hour.

Sid was nowhere to be seen, so I made a solitary walk to school, looking at the trees and feeling achy at the change of seasons. Jon always said autumn was his favorite because school started and trouble wasn't nearly as much fun to get into if you weren't ditching something. It was cool enough for mischief in the day, but still warm enough for mischief in the night, he'd claim with a wink and a whistle. He'd promised to teach me his special two-fingered high-low-high whistle, but we never got around to a lesson.

"I miss you an awful lot this morning, brother," I whispered to my marbles. I reached up and tugged on a tree branch, then let it go. I watched it bounce up and down in the sky, dancing between Heaven and earth. Leaves losing their green always got me a little hollow inside. It seemed unfair that they couldn't do a thing to keep from switching colors and then falling off altogether.

Fair to the trees or not, autumn had spread around St. Petersburg like wildfire, and the big oak looming over the back of Widow Douglas's house was leaking red and orange onto its leaves. The Widow's hound slumped over the front porch steps, licking his sore foreleg and fixing me with a stare. An enormous bone lay beside him, two feet long if it was an inch. It was too big to be anything but a cow bone from the butcher shop, but it was easy to imagine Charlemagne had swiped it from the graveyard.

I wondered if Mama would pay me any attention if I turned up as a pile of bones at the hands of the Pritchards.

Seeing the Pritchards on Saturday night had been a frightful thing indeed, but they were probably long gone by now. I could hear Jon's advice in my head: *There's a time to look out for marauders and then there's a time to steal from witches—get your head straight, Becky.*

Right where the path broke off toward the schoolhouse, a lone boy huddled over, tying one of his shoes. *Oh Lord.* I tried to hurry past Tom Sawyer, but he rose as I passed him, nearly poking me in the eye with his cowlick.

"Watch it," I said, waiting for him to get red and move.

Instead, he walked along next to me, grinning like a dumb old chicken headed to slaughter. "Hello, Becky. It's gonna be a fine day at school."

"Why's that?" I asked. "Did Mr. Dobbins tell you to clean the privy after you clean the chalkboard?" He'd do it too, just to get a pat on the head. What a goody-goody.

Before I could laugh at him, a thought dropped on me like a fallen acorn. I remembered what Amy had told me about why Sid and Tom lived with Aunt Polly. Maybe Tom thought if he was good enough, his daddy would get word and come back. If that was the case, poor Tom was wasting his time. I'd tried being real good and extra polite with Mama, but her heart and mind hadn't come back from wherever they'd gone to hide. There are certain things in life that go away and don't ever come back. Wishing or washing chalkboards can't make a lick of difference.

Before Tom could answer my privy question, we saw a crowd of boys and girls outside the schoolhouse. The air was abuzz with something, excited chatter and low murmurs floating among the elbows boys were digging into each others' sides.

I wormed my way past Sid Sawyer and the Green twins and found Amy. "What's all the ruckus about?" I asked her. But she didn't need to answer. Nailed right above the schoolhouse door was a shredded cloth and piece of paper.

I recognized the cloth and froze.

"What can it mean?" asked Rose Hobart. She clutched Sid's arm with her right hand while her left one fanned her chest.

"Somebody left it there for one of us—my money's on Tom," Sid said, ignoring the sickly shade of gray his brother was turning. He grinned and read the note aloud.

"TELL AND YULL BE RIPED TO SHREDS LIKE THIS HERE RAG."

My heartbeat banged extra hard in my chest, knocking against my lungs so I could hardly take a breath. That rag was the one Billy Pritchard had torn off me at the graveyard. He may not have known who I was, but he sure knew where to find me.

Settling my eyes on Amy, I searched her face for the same recognition, but she just looked puzzled. That was a weight off, knowing I would carry the burden alone (well, along with Tom Sawyer, who was convinced he was gonna get "riped" to shreds by somebody).

"'Riped' to shreds? That had to be Joe Harper," Ruth Bumpner declared, turning to Joe. "I could help you during the lunch hour if you want. You can't spell worth a darn."

"You can't look pretty worth a darn," Joe shot back, ignoring Ruth's hurt expression. "Wasn't me."

Tom looked downright terrified.

"Who'd you tell on this time?" Sid asked him.

"I don't rightly know," he rasped.

"Come on, Tom," I said, grabbing his hand and pulling him inside the schoolhouse. "That note's just a bad joke, that's all." Dropping his sweaty palm, I looked around the classroom. "Where's Dob-head, anyway?"

Tom pointed to the back door, where Mr. Sam Clemens was hanging his hat on the teacher's hook.

"What's he doing here?" I said louder than intended.

"*He's* playing teacher for the day," Sam said back. He smiled at the room, which was filling up and quieting down in the presence of a stranger. "Tom here got word at yesterday's church service that Mr. Dobbins was sick and school would be canceled for the day. He suggested I come to school so you didn't have to miss class, and his aunt thought that was a fine idea. Since I was getting nearly bored to sin waiting on that boat part to come in, I said why not." Turning to the chalkboard, he started to write his name. "Besides, it's bad manners to turn down the woman cooking your meals," he muttered with his back turned.

Three good-size spitballs smacked into Tom Sawyer's head from boys who would have rather missed class. Tom started to raise his hand to tattle on them, but a flick and evil eye from Sid stopped him.

Ruth Bumpner let out a harrumph in Sam's direction. "You're not a teacher, you're that steamboat pilot."

"I can't be a boat pilot with a grounded boat. Mr. Dobbins will be back tomorrow, so never you fear."

Ruth narrowed her eyes. "My mama saw you talking to the Widow Douglas. You were sitting right on her front porch."

Sam turned and nodded at her. "I needed something to curse the warts off my hands and heard she might be able to help. Cost me a dollar and a piece of my soul, but the warts are gone." He held up his hands, displaying clear palms.

Tom Sawyer craned his neck for a closer look. "I don't remember you having any wa—"

"Anyway, the name's Sam Clemens," Sam said, shooting Tom an annoyed glance, "and I wasn't always overly fond of my own schooling process, which I believe makes me qualified to teach. And while I despise subtraction, particularly when it comes to my own money, I do love to read and write. So we'll be talking about words all day."

"If you hate school, let's go have a fishing lesson," Joe Harper sang out. The other boys exchanged hesitant grins.

Sam clapped his hands and rubbed them together, taking a seat on the edge of Mr. Dobbins's desk. "Sure, we can go fishing. Or climb mountains or go dancing or play poker with elephants. We're gonna come up with a story and it can have as many adventures as you want."

Pinchy-face, not having any imagination to speak of, made her eyes into slits once again. "My mama says poker is the game of the devil."

"It is *not*," I told her, pocketing the dirty look she gave me so I could use it on her later. Jon was always partial to poker.

Joe Harper put on a sour pout. "I meant real fishing. I'm no story writer," he mumbled.

"No, but you're a liar," I pointed out. "That's all stories are— just a bunch of lies you think up and tell people." I peeked at Sam to see if he knew I was stealing his line.

"Tell you what," Sam said. "It's a nice day, so let's head down by the river to concoct our tale. Mr. Dobbins wouldn't object to a little fresh air, would he?"

I had a good spitball ready for Tom Sawyer, and the second he raised his hand to say that *yes*, Mr. Dobbins would surely throw a hissy fit if he knew we were doing anything that smelled of enjoyment, the wet wad of paper got him right on the neck.

"Hey," he said, turning in his seat.

"Let's go, everybody," I said, getting up.

And that's just what we did.

Amy and I kept toward the back of the group, her talking about what a lucky school day it was and me thinking about the "riped to shreds" note. The way I figured things, Billy Pritchard had done that to cover his behind and he wasn't likely to follow through on anything. Besides, I wasn't gonna say a word about them robbing that grave, which meant he'd have no reason to "ripe" me to shreds or otherwise. I brightened considerably at the revelation.

We passed the Widow's place and Pinchy-face's house. Mrs. Bumpner was in her front yard, all red-faced with both hands on her hips, frowning between her dead flower patch and the Widow's house and, now, the sight of Sam Clemens walking by.

Weaving along a river-bound path, me wishing I had Jon's overalls and a fishing pole, I soon realized our destination was somewhere near Sam's grounded steamboat. Sure enough, Sam settled on a log next to the burned-out fire pit where I'd first seen him. We all piled around him, the boys much distracted by a knife and candy wrappers a crew member had left behind.

"The Pritchards have been here," Sid said, waving the wrappers in Ruth's face.

She wrinkled her nose and shoved him away, but I felt Amy stiffen beside me.

"He's just foolin'," I told Amy, giving Sid the stink eye.

"He is not!" Joe Harper jumped on a log and pointed his finger at all of us. "See all the candy wrappers? Candy is probably the only thing those Pritchards eat and that's why they ain't got teeth left in their mouths."

"I wish you didn't have a mouth left in your mouth," Junie Todd told Joe.

I made a note to myself to get to know Junie better.

Sam laughed and pocketed the knife. "Hey now, that's just junk left over from river boys. Let's have a lesson," he said. All of us piped down and waited for him to tell us more. "The first thing you need for a story is characters and the second thing is something for them to do. Gimme a few names and we'll get started."

"Can we use real names?" Rose Hobart asked.

Sam nodded. "You can. Sometimes it's easier and more honest that way, especially if you're telling a tale with some truth to it. But it's fun to make them up, too. Now to start, we need a good fella and a bad one. Ideas for the good fella's name?"

"How about David," Tom suggested. "Like in the Bible story of David and—"

"Goliath!" Sid shouted. "Let's name our good guy Goliath."

Sam scribbled on his tablet. "All right, let's have a girl, too. Becky, any ideas?"

My stomach was grumbling too much for me to think.

I'd skipped out on seconds at breakfast. "Pancake Sally," I suggested.

"Good. Villain?"

"How about Mr. Lawrence." Pinchy-face smirked at Amy. "Never mind. He'd be stumbling around too much to do any damage." Her smug face changed to a serious kind of mean. "As my mother says," she whispered right to Amy, "what a waste of a family."

Even Mary and Alice Green had the sense to look shocked, and they were friends with Ruth.

A wad of tears gathered in Amy's eyes. Her fingers clutched my side, holding me back from leaping up and giving Ruth a whooping in front of God and Sam Clemens and everyone.

"Don't," Amy whispered, wiping at her cheek with a fierce swipe. "She's not worth it."

I disagreed. I thought Ruth Bumpner was very much worth a few of my scraped knuckles, if it was her nose doing the scraping. *Waste of a family.* That was it—now the whole Bumpner family had made it onto my special list.

"I got a villain. How about Mr. Dobbins!" Joe shouted gleefully, prompting those around him to applaud.

Sam laughed, but shook his head. "You can do better than that."

So with Sam Clemens pointing to each of us in turn to shout out a sentence of story, Goliath and Pancake Sally had soon defeated the evil Mr. Smobbins by tying him to a raft and sending him downriver where he was subjected to torture by the Gritchard brothers, the most terrible pirates known to sail the Mississippi. Just as the Gritchards were going to hunt down Goliath and Pancake Sally as well, Hurricane Mo, Goliath's long-lost brother, entered the scene. We broke for lunch, with three young lives hanging in the balance.

Amy and I found a nice tree to set our backs to, speculating about Hurricane Mo's chances of saving the day while we poked holes in four lima beans each.

"This'll give us protection from the north, south, east, and west," I said, passing her a piece of fishing line. "String your beans on that and we'll stick the necklaces in this Bible." I patted the Good Book. "Then we'll take turns sitting on it."

Amy's eyes filled with a considerable amount of reproach. "Isn't it an awful sin, sitting on the Bible?"

"Course not," I told her, finishing my necklace with a fishing knot. "It puts you that much closer to God, doesn't it? And it'll squeeze the Holiness right into those beans. Jon once snatched six watermelons with the help of holy beans."

Amy let out a soft sigh, accepting half of my ham on white bread. "Must've been nice having a brother. When did Jon die?"

Nobody had asked me anything about him in a real long time. Felt nice to hear his name from someone else. "End of last summer." It'd been the beginning of August, just short of his favorite season. I sure hoped God had changed it to look like autumn in Heaven the day Jon died, so he felt good and welcomed.

"How'd he die? Mama died from pneumonia. I nearly caught it, but I'm not carrying it around with me or anything." She looked at me anxiously.

"I'm sure you're not," I assured her, taking her hand in mine to let her know I wasn't scared of old pneumonia germs. "Say, if you feel like someone's gonna make you sick, know what you do?"

Amy's eyeballs got real wide. "What do I do?"

A memory flashed of Jon in his bed, frail and faded, weakly whispering his secrets to me. Like he was already a ghost. I changed the memory and put some color into his cheeks. "That's better."

"What's better?"

"Nothing." I leaned against the tree, trying to remember exactly what Jon had said. "Here's what you do. You go outside and find something living in the ground. Could be a flower, a piece of grass, or a worm. Harder to find living things in winter, but you got to anyway. Then you bring the thing inside, dip it in flour, and fry it in oil."

"You don't eat it!" Amy cried.

"You *do* eat it! But not yet. First you find the darkest room in the house. That's usually a closet. You take a glass of water and your fried living thing in there and you spin around twice one way, twice the other, then sit down and take your salt. Did I mention the salt?"

She shook her head.

"You need a quarter cup of salt. And a glass of water. You sit down and you pour the salt into the cup. You stir it around with a dirty spoon. Did I mention the dirty spoon?"

She shook her head again. "What if they're all clean?"

"Then you drop one on the floor a few times or shove it under the cook stove."

Amy wrinkled her nose. "It's got to be dirty?"

I nodded firmly. "*Got* to be. Anyway, you stir the salt into the water and say,

Salt water, fried thing, do your best,
Don't let sickness jump in my chest,
Pollywog, johnnycake, syrup in your eye,
I'll drink you, if you don't let me die."

Amy waited for more. "Then what?"

"Then you eat your fried living thing and swallow all the salt water."

She frowned. "Does that really work, Becky Thatcher?"

Finishing off my sandwich, I shook the crumbs from my dress. "I didn't get sick, did I?"

"Well, could it have helped my mama? Ooo, skitter on your neck!"

I slapped the sneaky bloodsucker, wiping my hand on my fishskin and hoping the stain would make it unwearable. Maybe Mama would give me a scolding if she ever came close enough to notice. I mushed the body around real good, just in case.

"No," I told Amy, "that chant couldn't have helped your Mama. Jon said it doesn't do any good if you're already sick. That's how he died. Just got sick. Then he got sicker. Couldn't even come down to the stream to fish. He said that he would've skipped school every day he'd ever gone if he knew he'd be seventeen and too weak for running around the woods. Told me that he would have had adventures all over the place." I stuck my hand inside my schoolbag, touching his marble bag. "Said he would have gone all the way to the ocean."

Amy shifted beside me. "Is that why you act wild sometimes and wear his clothes?"

If anybody else had asked me that, I might have got

offended, but Amy was my bosom friend. "Miss Ada thinks that I want to be like him." I dug my shoes into the ground. "I miss him so much some days that my chest hurts, Amy. It feels like someone's just pressing and squeezing on me. But if I put on a shirt of his, it's like he's the one holding me instead, doing the squeezing his own self." I scraped my fingers along the tree, feeling the bark get good and lodged under my fingernails. "He used to pick me up from the floor and call me a daisy."

"He called you what?"

"He called me Daisy." I started to feel sniffly and needed something else to talk about. "Your kitten dead yet?" Immediately, I regretted the question. Amy looked ready to bawl and school is no place for crying. "Never mind," I said. "Don't tell me. But hey, think about it like this—if it dies, that kitten'll get the glory of helping us."

She looked at me strange for a second, then sighed. "Oh, Becky, maybe you're right. I sure do feel bad, though. He looks near about dead. I even tried soaking one of Daddy's holey socks in milk and feeding him that way, but nothing worked."

"That's too bad," I said. "Say, when it dies, you can keep that dead kitten in your room until we need its witch-repelling powers. Maybe keep it on your bed pillow. Then it would feel nice and taken care of." I smiled real big to show her how kind that would be.

Her mouth twitched like she was in pain or she'd eaten a bad piece of fish. "What if it's got maggots?"

"You pick 'em out."

Amy still looked a little sick, but she nodded. "You're right." I clapped her on the back. "Sure I am."

Down by the river, Sam Clemens waved his hands and shouted for us to gather back together. The Mississippi was busy with freight boats and fishing skiffs mingling together, making a much nicer background for learning than a chalkboard. In a fit of bad manners, I found myself wishing that Mr. Dobbins would stay good and sick so we could have riverside school again tomorrow.

I stood and reached for Amy's hand. "Let's go see how the story turns out."

"I hope those boys and Sally get away," she said, picking up the Bible. "I don't want to hear about anybody getting their toes sliced off by Gritchards. I don't much like this story."

"No," I agreed, "me neither." That said, I was very glad that nobody had thrown a dug-up grave scene into the mix.

Because while the class and Sam Clemens were busy thinking up pretend pirates and pretend torture and pretend escapes, I was thinking how somebody was bound to go to the cemetery sooner or later and find a real live dead body.

Chapter Eight

———•———

A rumored suspect

The unearthed coffin of Mr. Amos Mutton was discovered three days after the grave robbing, and the story
spread easy as warm butter. It was a curiosity, since Mr. Mutton
had died five years back, and nobody knew of him being buried
with anything particularly valuable. Preacher Sprague swore
he'd been at the funeral and that not a thing went into that
coffin except a body wearing pants, suspenders, a shirt, and
new socks that someone had been kind enough to knit. It was
the Church who buried him out of kindness, him not having a
wife. The body still being there and Amos being fully clothed
and such, it was a most mysterious happening.

Every ounce of Law available surveyed the scene. Even
Daddy was called to the graveyard to take a look on Tuesday
afternoon. Amy and I kept our mouths shut tight. If the
Pritchard brothers wanted to dig up some man who was

already dead, it wasn't worth us getting our guts spilled with that big knife of Billy's. Amy and I were firmly against any of our body parts taking leave of our bodies.

But there was a complication—a big one, in the form of my six-foot-tall-and-then-some Daddy sitting down at the kitchen table to make conversation on Wednesday morning over hotcakes, eggs, and bacon.

I helped myself to the pans on the cookstove, scooping up eggs and all the bacon that was left and taking a seat next to my daddy.

"Becky." He nodded, pointing for me to pass the syrup.

"Yes, Daddy," I said cautiously, digging into my food and wondering why he didn't want to eat in the dining room again. Maybe it was because Miss Ada was out back with the washing and he didn't want to travel as far for seconds. Maybe he also liked it better in the kitchen since there wasn't an empty Mama chair to stare at. "You eating breakfast again?" I asked him.

"My stomach has taken to being soured by plain coffee, and I wanted to speak with you. Becky, I know you've made friends with Amy Lawrence, but have you gotten to know the Bumpner girl?"

Oh. Well, that was unexpected. "No, I have *not* gotten acquainted with Ruth Bumpner," I said, being diplomatic. "Why?"

He took a big bite of hotcake and chewed with his mouth wide open. Daddy had gotten away with rude table manners since Mama stopped talking enough to chide him. "Her parents are issuing a complaint of sorts, and I don't know what to think of the family. Hard to ask questions without offending people in a small town. What about the Sawyer boys? Do you find them to be agreeable?"

Hmm. Where was Daddy going with this? Did he know about the witchy bet?

"The Sawyers seem very nice, Daddy. Sid's more friendly than Tom. I'll say that."

"They ever mention that fellow living with them?"

This was about *him.* Whew, what a relief! I relaxed and drowned a piece of bacon in my syrup pool. "Sam Clemens? He's the pilot of that grounded steamboat. He's waiting on an engine part, I guess. He's a writer, too. Seems friendly. Why?" That bacon with syrup went down like candy. Mmm.

"Well, word around town is that he's been seen talking to the Widow Douglas."

A hotcake wad went down the wrong pipe and I choked a few times before recovering. I didn't like talk turning to the Widow Douglas. Did Sam Clemens turn into Tom Sawyer and tattle about the bet? I didn't say anything. Daddy hadn't asked a question, so I waited.

"A shovel the deputy found at the grave of Mr. Mutton was traced to the Widow. It's the same red-tipped one she gardens with."

Good Lord, there went another chunk down the wrong pipe. *The Pritchards had stolen the Widow's shovel.* Not that I wouldn't be participating in a bet that involved lifting an item from the Widow's house on Saturday, but those were two very different things. That was for bragging rights and there was a five dollar pot at stake. "You think the Widow dug up that grave?"

He shook his head. "It seems unlikely, but Mr. Bumpner heard about the shovel being found. He and his wife came to see me personally and said that the Widow's not quite right in the head. She doesn't attend church, keeps to herself a lot. Said they'd testify to her oddities if she went to trial."

Just because a witch is a witch doesn't mean I want people sending her to jail for something she never did. That's just plain mean. I stood up fast. "Went to trial? But she didn't have anything to do with that grave robbery!" I clapped a hand over my mouth and waited for Daddy to ask how I could know such a thing.

He did not. Instead he did something worse. He sighed at me. "Sit down, Becky. There's no need to be so dramatic. We're just going to ask her a few questions. That's all we're doing at this point."

I sat back in my chair and waited. There *was* a need to be dramatic, what with an innocent witch being questioned like a criminal. *Well, shoot.* My pesky conscience was tapping at me like a woodpecker, making me think maybe I should just up and tell what I'd seen at the graveyard.

"Seems the Law also found evidence of a large dog pawing around. Prints the size of a grown woman's hand. The Widow's dog is mighty big."

He sure is. I dunked a piece of bacon in the remaining puddle of syrup, sliding it back and forth, trying to think of a way to tell Daddy what I saw at the cemetery without getting in trouble for sneaking out or putting my family and Amy's in danger with the outlaws. "So the deputy and sheriff both think the Widow did it?"

"Sheriff wants to talk to her, that's all. Wants to talk to the writer, too."

"But they haven't been arrested for anything yet, right?" My morals were twitching, hoping for a loophole out of tattling on the Pritchards and myself. It was a mighty enough struggle to keep my mouth shut about the outlaws being near town, but now I had the Widow's fate resting on me as well. What was the responsible thing to do? I had to admit that, most likely, a responsible girl wouldn't have found herself collecting dirt in a cemetery in the first place. *Too late for that.* Maybe the better question was: What would Jon do in my situation?

"No one's been arrested for anything, but people want to see someone judged for what happened. Folks don't like bodies being dug up."

The Widow wouldn't get in real trouble just from being questioned, I reasoned. She'd just tell the sheriff that she wasn't at the cemetery that night. If that didn't work, she could put a spell on everyone until they believed her. Easy-peasy. My morals settled down.

"Daddy, they didn't find anything else at the graveyard?" *Like two girl-size hidey spots under a blackberry bush.*

"No."

"What about the Pritchards?" I asked real casual. "Any news about them?"

"Word came this morning. The Pritchard brothers seem to have skipped past these parts and headed south to Trittsville, thank the Lord. They hit a bank and then busted up a sweet shop for the heck of it."

Trittsville. At the graveyard, Billy had said something about going to Trittsville and coming back afterward. Did he mean back to St. Petersburg?

Daddy sighed again, staring at my plate. "Stop dredging your bacon through the syrup like you're drowning a cat."

I stopped. That was exactly what he used to say to Jon.

"Becky, honey, you need to start acting like a grown-up. No more playing with your food and running around with Sid Sawyer. You're too old to be spitting cherries with boys."

I felt my head get hot. I supposed Tom Sawyer had told someone about that, too.

"And *stop* wearing your brother's old clothes. I saw them swinging from the laundry line earlier this week, so I know you've been up to something."

Darn it. Miss Ada didn't mind me wearing Jon's shirts and pants. Heck, she was the one who put all his clothes in a trunk when he died and let me know where the key was. "Maybe Miss Ada just likes to clean them. She was always partial to Jon."

"I'm tired, Becky. I'm tired of repeating myself. I've got things I should be thinking about other than your childish mischief."

Hmph. What he really meant is that he had better things to be thinking about than me. That even thinking about me was becoming a burden, just like it was to Mama. My fingers itched to hit something. "You know Mama doesn't attend church. Some people might say she's not right in the head, either. She on your list of suspects? Sheriff going to haul her in for questions?"

Daddy fixed me with his judge look. "Becky Thatcher, I'm ashamed of what just left your mouth. Don't you talk about your mama that way. She suffers enough without you speaking poorly about her."

My cheeks burned even hotter, like someone had lit a firecracker in my mouth. He was ashamed of *me*? What about Mama, who hadn't done a single thing to fit in around St. Petersburg? Who hadn't done a single thing to show that she still had a child alive.

Somehow, I forced myself into a humble position with my head down and hands in my lap. I shook in anger and from holding my tongue, but it probably worked to my advantage, making it seem like I was about to cry. Which I was *not* about to do.

"Yes, Judge. I'm sorry and I'll surely try harder."

Daddy stood and checked Old Reliable (which I'd been real careful about putting back in Daddy's office by church time on Sunday). He loomed over me and the table for a moment, then pushed his chair in, leaving a good couple slices of bacon on his plate. "Have a good day at school, sweetheart."

I watched him go before swiping the bacon from his plate and slipping it into the special dress pocket Miss Ada had sewn for me, adding it to the three pieces I'd already hid away. I told Miss Ada I needed a pocket because of my tendency to lose writing chalk, which was the truth, though it came in handy to hold other things more often than not. Charlemagne was a mighty big dog, and Amy and I'd need all the help we could get in sneaking past him Saturday night.

Miss Ada entered the dining room and picked up my plate, sticking me to the wall with her eyeballs. She must have heard what I said about Mama.

I kept my eyes down and picked at the scab on my knee, afraid to look up at her.

Gently, she cupped my chin in her hand and tilted my head up to meet hers. "You leave that scab alone, you hear me? Keep picking and picking at something like that, making it bleed over and over, and your whole leg will be ruined. Knees and hearts take enough bruising from life as it is. They ain't meant to be beat up by your own self."

I nodded and dropped my hands into my lap.

"You gonna be late for school if you don't hurry."

"I'm going." I gathered my things, hanging my head low.

"Your mama's gonna come around," Miss Ada said. "She just needs time."

"I got other things to think about besides Mama."

And I did have other things. In three days, Amy and I would be taking part in the boys' bet and there wasn't much glory in swiping an item from the empty house of an arrested and jailed witch. The only evidence that the sheriff had in his possession pointed to the Widow. Amy and I were the only two people in town who could vouch for her. There had to be some way to prove that Widow Douglas wasn't at the grave-yard, without incriminating ourselves.

On the way out the back door, I caught sight of our own garden shovel propped against the house near our side garden. Miss Ada had been putting in autumn mums. Picturing the splash of color the flowers would make, an idea hit me like a rogue skitter bite. Maybe I couldn't stop the sheriff from asking questions around town, but I might be able to delay any arrests.

Nodding to myself, I walked to school and fixed my head with plans that were certain to keep the Widow out of jail for at least another couple of days.

I shared my plans and Daddy's news with Amy during lunch and she was eager to help. When Dob-head had finished sneering at us for the day, we headed to the Lawrence place for supplies. Lucky for us, she had a bucket of paint that was real close to the red we needed and a shovel her daddy would never miss. After brushing the tip of the shovel's handle with a few coats and letting it dry, I took the tool and paint home with me. I hid them in our shed behind a set of flower pots.

That night, once Daddy was in bed, I changed into overalls and snuck out to stash Amy's shovel under the Widow's wraparound porch. Hoping my kind intentions would cancel out any witchy no-trespassing curses she'd placed around the house, I knew I was doing the right thing. The authorities had possession of a shovel they *thought* was the Widow's, but I'd just provided evidence to the contrary. Widow Douglas's shovel could be found good and settled in her own yard.

Taking a roundabout way home to shake off any of the Widow Witch's spirit helpers, I passed by the Bumpner house, and a fat ham of a thought occurred to me. The Bumpners had some trouble owed to them for being mean in general and to Amy Lawrence in particular. I had just the right manner of justice in mind. I fetched the paint and brush from my house, then ran back to Pinchy-face's property.

Their house was completely dark, so I walked right over to the shed in the backyard. The inside was neatly organized and

I got straight to work, giving a good two coats to the handle tips of a hoe, spade, and rake. The tool set looked just like the Lawrences'. I bet Ruth would be embarrassed to know she and Amy had something in common, even if it only was a tool from Marley's Dry Goods Emporium.

Only when I reached for a bucket containing garden trowels did I see a special something—a leather-bound booklet tucked down into a corner crack sweet as you please. Thumbing through the pages, I could hardly keep from hooting like an owl when I realized what kind of treasure I'd found.

I didn't have much time to wander through Ruth's hidden journal entries, but one caught my eye and made me suck in a wad of air thick as a brick.

> Oh Joe Harper, you should ~~see~~, know,
> I love you more ~~than sugar cookie~~
> ~~dough my velvet~~ bow
> fresh white snow,
> Your ~~cheeks~~ ears are freckled sweet,
> your eyes so shiny bright,
> I wish that I could ~~make you miney~~
> ~~hold~~ squeeze you tight.

It took every ounce of strength not to let out a laugh that would wake the whole Pinchy-face family. It was even funnier since I was certain Joe hated Ruth, and I was pretty sure he sort of liked Amy. I put the journal snugly in my front overall pocket, my mind spinning with ways I might put such interesting information to good and revengeful use. With a muffled snort, I slapped a quick two coats on the trowels and made my way home. On the way I took the liberty of relocating the Bumpners' plain shovel to a hidden spot in the woods, where nobody would find it. Mighty pleased with myself as I crept back into bed, I patted my marble sack and thought of my brother.

"Just you wait, Jon. This Saturday'll be quite the show."

Chapter Nine

––––—•—––––

My marbles in danger
(and I hate, hate, hate Mr. Dobbins)

When I came down to breakfast Thursday morning, my nerves were up and alert despite the rest of me feeling dog tired. Daddy was stabbing at fried eggs and reading through a stack of papers at the kitchen table. Covering a series of yawns, I stepped aside while Miss Ada nudged past me with a single hotcake and egg on a plate. Creaking stairs told me where she was headed. I sat down to a breakfast of steaming hotcakes and syrup, hearing three knocks on an upstairs door. A jealous part of me hoped Mama wouldn't answer.

But the door opened with a soft click and Miss Ada came down empty handed. My chest tightened for a minute and I felt something sore behind my eyes. Maybe I'd given myself a cold by being out the night before.

"Morning, Daddy." One of his papers was sticking out from the rest and I saw the word "Reward." It sent a prickle through my body all the way to my feet, making my toes tap on the floor. "Are those papers about the Pritchards?"

He took a sip of coffee. "Yep. Sheriff's trying to decide whether or not to take the posters down around town. I told him there's not much use in getting people nervous if the Pritchards have gone downriver for good."

I swallowed hard, trying to get a wad of guilt back down in my stomach before it could pop out of my mouth and say something that would get me in trouble. Besides, I needed to concentrate on the Widow Douglas this morning, not the Pritchards. "You still busy with that dug-up grave business?"

"Mm-hm," he said, chewing and not looking up. The dining chair creaked beneath his considerable frame and I wondered if Daddy getting a breakfast appetite might be bad news for the furniture.

"Seems awful odd that the sheriff found the Widow's shovel at the graveyard when I saw it clear as day underneath her porch on my walk home from school yesterday." I took a big bite and chewed, waiting for his reaction.

"Odd," he echoed, eyes still glued to his paperwork. "Well, the Bumpners were mighty quick to let us know it was the Widow's shovel, so maybe she's got two."

I shrugged, trying to ignore the faces of Billy and Forney Pritchard glaring at me from Daddy's stack. "Maybe." I put down a forkful of hotcake. "Now *that's* funny."

Daddy squinted like he had a headache, but put his fork down and watched me. "What's funny?"

"Well, if I recall, the Bumpners have red handles on *their* tool set too. I saw Mrs. Bumpner working on that awful garden of hers last week." Which was true enough. I'd seen her. "I could have sworn that her pruning shears and hoe had red tips on the handles. I'm pretty sure, anyway. Might want to check and see if their shovel is accounted for." I took another bite. "Maybe I'm wrong. These hotcakes sure are tasty."

Daddy stared at me for a good minute, but I didn't look up from my food. Then he stood, checked the wall clock, and grabbed for his hat.

"Going to work?" I asked. "It's a little early."

"I have a feeling it might be a long day," he muttered, leaving the back door open on his way out.

Maybe I should have felt bad about hauling the Bumpners into the mess, but I was confident they'd whine their way out of blame. And the whole shovel business had sparked an idea. If I could find a way to lead the sheriff to the Pritchards without information coming right from me, maybe I could avoid getting punished for sneaking out to the cemetery. The problem was, I couldn't say for sure where the Pritchards might be. According to Daddy, they were downriver and our sleepy town was safe as a baby crib. Maybe he was right.

Mr. Dobbins had been awful mean lately (even for him), and school was a terrible burden to get through that week. He was jittery, that's what it was, and sick, too. He sounded all stuffed up and sneezed a lot, letting the spray hit whoever was closest. A jittery, smelly teacher is a dangerous thing, especially when he's jammed into a one-room schoolhouse with boys and girls who'd rather be out enjoying the day. By Friday afternoon, the only person not scrambling for one of the seats in the back was Tom Sawyer.

Being warned by his extra-crusty behavior, I should have known better and just paid attention in class. But Mr. Dobbins got to yelling about spelling again, and that's something I pride myself on. He droned on and on, occasionally snapping at young ones for getting their *K*'s and *C*'s mixed up.

Sid sat in front of me, and I saw that he was drawing a picture and trying to show it to Rose Hobart. I peeked. It was a house. A pretty good drawing, too. There in the house's yard, Sid had drawn a stick man and a stick lady holding hands. Rose giggled and patted the man on the head.

All of a sudden, I felt awful mad. The nerve of Sid! What would he go and like Rose Hobart for anyway? She wouldn't be the type to take the witch's bet or wear overalls or let Joe Harper pick her scab. Why, she was no fun at all. Too grown-up for her own good, that's what she was. And *responsible*, which was just another way of saying someone was dull as plain grits.

I bet he was planning on walking with her that afternoon, after he and Joe went to get sand. Sid and Joe thought they were so smart. I overheard them at lunch talking about getting a few bucketfuls of Mississippi sandbar right after school. I think Amy told them about our protective dirt, and they were getting worried about their own defenses.

Poor idiots. Sand didn't have any protective powers unless you piled it around three dead frogs and said the right words, which I guessed they didn't know. Even if they did know the right words, you can't gather protective sand in the daylight. Any fool knows that.

Never mind Sid. Amy Lawrence was my bosom friend and

I resolved right then and there to write a nice note reminding her of just that.

"Sid Sawyer!"

While Sid got hauled up and roughly thwapped with a fly swatter for drawing pictures during class, I scratched a note on a piece of paper and threw it over to Amy. She sat on the outside edge of her row again, which was most convenient for note tossing.

Mr. Dobbins must have sensed the note flying through the air, because he paused mid-thwap. His head jerked around the room like a bloodhound looking for a steak trail.

I made myself busy and innocent by pulling out my marble bag. I shifted it in my hand, took one marble out, put it back, took another one out, put it back. There's nothing like doing something else, something a little *less* bad for excusing yourself from the badder thing you've done.

"Amy Lawrence!"

My heartbeat echoed in my ears, and I felt my face get hot. Not my Amy!

"Ye-es, sir?"

"Who threw something across my classroom?"

"I don't know, sir. I reckon I was working on my sums." She held up her chalkboard and displayed *47+74=121*.

Excellent! My lying lessons had gone over like cream on peaches.

Dobbins strode around the room and each child he asked claimed to know nothing. Their eyes had all been dutifully on the switching going on up front. When he got to Pinchy-face, who sat next to me, I got a little nervous. She had an awful grin on her face and seemed ready to tell on me, but a sharp poke with my pencil tip convinced her otherwise.

"This is ridiculous!" Mr. Dobbins bellowed. He breathed in and out of his nose, spraying flecks of deep-seated dried nostril snot and looking madder than I'd ever seen him. Mean mad. "I hate this job." He marched back and forth in a tight line at the front of the classroom, huffing like a cornered bull. "And I'm not letting all this disrespect pass, you hear? I'm an educated man! I'm a dentist!"

The room went dead quiet. Nobody even dared to scratch an itch.

Our teacher's voice became dangerously soft. "You're all just evil scraps of decaying cow, trying to disease me with your filthy childhoods. No, you're not the scraps. You're the maggots in the scraps, and I pray to God I won't have to deal with you much longer."

The silence continued, this time in appreciation of his insult. That was a darn good one. *Maggots in the scraps.* I'd have to tuck that one away and tell it to Jon that evening. Mr. Dobbins was wrong about not having to deal with us much longer, though. The youngest students had at least another seven or eight years of school.

Finally, there was one person he hadn't questioned about the note. When old Dob-head's eyes lit onto Tom Sawyer, I suspected I was doomed. Searching my mind for anything to stop what was coming, I slyly reached down for a matchbox of salt I kept in my school satchel in case I brought hard-boiled eggs for lunch. Sliding it open, I pinched some crystals between two fingers and tossed them toward Dob's feet. As I did, I caught a glimpse of his sock.

It had a solid brown stain on it that I recognized as dried blood. Whatever injury he'd gotten was probably breaking open every time he took a step. Secretly, I hoped a whole wad of skitters found their way into that wound at night and laid themselves some eggs. While I relished that image, I clutched my bag of marbles and said a protective verse in my head.

> *Little pinch o' salt toward a big man's feet,*
> *Criny-ho, criny-ho, raw sack o' meat*
> *Chicken head on a stick, straw in his nose,*
> *Make a man deaf with salt between his toes.*

Jon said that salt was good for sprinkling on Daddy and Mama's toes before he would sneak out. The chant was meant more to keep a sleeping man asleep than to make a teacher deaf against hearing a school boy tattling, but it was all I could think of. I hoped it would work. If not, my fate depended on Tom Sawyer's answer.

Dobbins placed both hands on Tom's desk. "Who did it? You got such a nice record in school, Tom. I hate to tell Aunt Polly you were dishonest with me."

Little beads of sweat dotted Tom's forehead, and he was breathing hard. Strangely enough, it looked like he was uncomfortable with having to tattle on someone. His shoulders lifted and then dropped.

My goodness! Tom Sawyer just *shrugged* at Mr. Dobbins. Maybe I wasn't doomed after all . . .

Dob-head leaned closer, so he was nose-to-nose with Tom.

"I'll ask you one more time, Tom Sawyer." His fist came down on the desktop. "*Who* was it?"

With a whimper, Tom shifted in his seat and pointed a shaky finger my way.

Rascal. Should've known better.

"And what exactly was that, floating through the air, hmm?"

"I reckon . . ." Tom's voice cracked on the word "reckon" and he paused to take a deep breath.

A few low snickers rang out like sirens. I waited, wondering why Tom Sawyer'd been looking at me in the first place when he should've been watching his brother get fly-swatter-whipped. I'd have to ask about that when I gave him a thumping later.

"*What?*"

"M-maybe she was passing a note?"

Dobbins's beady eyes gleamed. He looked like a fox licking his chops before pouncing on a chicken. "Passing a note to who, Tom?"

The room was silent, and I could see Tom's shoulders trembling. He dipped his head down until it rested in his hands.

"*Who?!*"

Even I knew what Tom would do, and for once I wasn't about to place the blame only on him. It was a cruel trap for Dobbins to set for someone with Tom's weak character—someone who knew he was only popular with adults and who desperately wanted to hold on tight to somebody, anybody, liking him. Even if it was old Dob-head.

I felt sorry for Tom Sawyer at that moment. I did. It's a hard thing coming to a new town and only making a few friends, but it must be a harder thing to already be in a town and have no friends at all.

I raised my hand. "It *was* me, sir. I tossed a note, but it wasn't to anybody. I was trying for a magic trick," I lied. "Making the paper disappear and all. Sorry to have done it on school time." *Whew*. Now Amy couldn't get in trouble. If that wasn't a responsible use of a lie, I don't know what was. I almost wished Daddy was there to witness such responsibility on my part.

Dobbins's eyes searched the floor, then moved to the faces of everyone on the right side of the room. "And where is this note?"

Shooting up, I scanned the floor. Then I squatted down to check under seats. Knowing perfectly well that note was tucked in Amy Lawrence's sleeve, I bounced twice and let out a whoop. "Yahoo! By Heaven and all that's holy, it worked!" I thought it was mighty clever, me saying the note disappeared (thereby protecting Amy) *and* fitting in a reminder of holy things at the same time (so he'd feel bad about beating someone so religious).

"What's that?" He pointed to the bag of Jon's marbles still clutched in my hand.

"Nothing." I placed the bag behind my back and wagged it at Joe Harper, but he either wasn't paying attention or was too dumb, 'cause he didn't snatch it from me.

Instead, Dobbins hauled me up front and gave me an ear flick. An *ear flick*! That was my punishment! I reckon some mama told him not to be striking girls, but he felt like it was open season on flicks. Well, I was fine and dandy with that. He couldn't knock a dead fly off a windowsill with that weak finger. In fact, I was sorely tempted to give him one back just to show him how it was done, but I just rubbed on my ear and fixed myself with a pained expression.

Jon and I used to have finger flicking wars. This one particular flicking war of ours from three or four years ago, I was sitting on a log by the fish pond back in Riley, enjoying the sunshine and hoping for a bite, when out of nowhere a solid thwap set one of my ears to ringing. It was such a shock that I thought maybe someone was slingshotting rocks my way, so I jumped straight in the water to hide behind some catty tails. Jon had laughed and laughed, then jumped in after me, and we had a water flicking war, and then went and pinched a watermelon from Mr. Hannibal's farm down the road. What a day that was.

The memory made Dobbins's flick even easier to take, but what happened next was a most painful tragedy. Dobbins grabbed my leather bag and dug through Jon's marbles.

"Please, sir," I pleaded, against my nature. "I'll put them clean away! I was just holding them, not doing anything, I promise! They're not even to play with in the dirt or anything. They're just to look at."

It made my skin crawl to see that man placing his greasy meanie fingers on my marbles. The truth was, they were much more than marbles. A spirit man my brother was acquainted with had come over shortly before Jon died. Mama and Daddy were at some town meeting and I let him in the house. He did a chant on Jon's best marbles, putting a little piece of my brother inside them. It was Jon's idea to do it. We made sure the spirit man sent most all of Jon's soul straight to Heaven, but Jon said he wasn't done having adventures yet. He said I could take his marbles everywhere and he'd be able to feel the adventure from way up in the sky.

"These are interesting. Bet they're very special to you." Dob-head said the word "special" all slimy, not the respectful way that Sam Clemens had. He held up a tiger's eye one and a blue one painted with a fish. Then he started walking over to his desk.

I knew just what he aimed to do. "No! Mr. Dobbins, please, no!" Leaping across the floor, I grabbed his elbow, but he shook me off with a growl and shoved me away. Taking a key from his pocket, he unlocked the bottom drawer.

Inside was a heaping load of confiscated treats, some funny-looking house tools, a tiny coil of wire and . . . shiny corn kernels? Seemed odd. Was Mr. Dobbins wanting to be a farmer? According to Sid, Dobbins boarded at the Green twins' place and didn't have any land, just a room.

Quick as a whip, Dob-head scooted those kernels to the back, stuck Jon's marbles inside, and slammed the drawer shut.

With a twist of his wrist, the drawer was locked.

Chapter Ten

---·---

Stealing from the Widow Witch Douglas

A t ten thirty the next evening I was still fuming over the loss of my marbles, but was also considerably occupied by our plan of thievery. Daddy had left for his town office after supper, shaking his head and mumbling about rogue garden tools, and Mama was hiding in her room again, so sneaking out wasn't any trouble. Still, I was a little nervous about venturing into the night when the Pritchards could be prowling around St. Petersburg, and by the time Amy appeared at my back fence, I'd gnawed through two stale pieces of the bacon stolen from Wednesday's breakfast. But a bet was a bet.

"You got the dead cat?" I asked Amy.

She lifted a flour sack. "Right here. I feel real bad about it."

I straightened the too-big overalls on her shoulders. "Well, don't. That kitten's already up in Heaven rolling balls of yarn around. What you got there is nothing but a body." I gave it a little finger poke to prove it.

Amy chewed her lips and watched the sack sway side to side. "You think it'll help?"

"Sure it will. I fear greatly for Joe and Sid, not having a dead cat and midnight dirt. Now, tuck your hair up under that hat," I said, pushing my braids beneath my own hat and giving a pat to my overall pocket, wishing it was full of Jon's marbles instead of grave dirt.

The pair I wore had a green patch on the front pocket. Jon had once caught seven creek frogs and stuck them inside that pocket. He ran home with both hands holding the frogs to his chest and called me to grab a hat box from Mama's room to keep them all in. Before I could hurry to find one, Mama bustled into the parlor and surprised us. Jon rushed for the back door, but slipped on a rug and fell. The frogs flew out, and by the time he pried himself off the floor, every one of his prisoners had escaped, plus he'd torn the pocket on a sticking-up floor nail. It took four hours to find all those slimy frogs. Mama eventually calmed down and sewed the pocket patch herself, using green fabric. I touched the stitches, remembering how she'd laughed when she told Daddy what happened.

We set off for the Widow's house, taking the stream trail so we'd come up on her backyard from the woods. A night owl that was diving for prey flew right past us, reminding me that we weren't alone and making me wonder if I shouldn't have warned our competitors that the Pritchard brothers could be lurking about. I hadn't thought about that, and the sudden sense of guilt made my armpits slick with sweat.

Chances at five dollars and adventure don't come along every day, Jon would have told me. *Either get your head on right or go peck in the corn with the chickens, little sister.*

There was no sign of Sid and Joe, nor any of the others. We figured it was best to get first shift, before anyone spooked the Widow with noise. Besides, eleven o'clock was late enough for an older lady to be sleeping, witch or no witch.

The house looked dark enough. Unlike the week before, there wasn't a single sign of rain, just a sliver of early October moonlight. We crept to the river side of the Widow's place, where I noticed a henhouse and small scratching yard for the first time.

"I didn't figure on witchy chickens, so be extra quiet around that henhouse. First we've got to scatter the grave dirt on every side," I whispered. "We'll start here and work our way around to the back. Take a handful of dirt and repeat after me:

Graveyard dirt from a bad man's plot,
Make our stealin' hard to spot."

Amy repeated the phrase four times, gaining confidence as we snuck around the property. "What now?" she asked in a high, breathless voice. Her eyes were bright and she was bouncing foot to foot.

I was pleased to see her excited. "There's an open window on the back porch." I pointed. "Let's go."

"Maybe we could reach right in and snag a doily, without ever stepping foot inside. That's *it*, Becky." She gripped my arm, squeezing hard. "And we'll shut the window after, so the boys don't get a chance to use it!"

I was doubly pleased to see her thinking ahead like that. "Perfect. We're just about ready. Put your hands out."

She dropped the dead kitten on the ground and held up her palms.

"We're gonna slap four times, then spit over each other's shoulder."

"Four times, then spit," she repeated. "Why four?"

"Everyone knows that three, which is usually a handy number for protection and such, doesn't do nothing in the case of thievery and pirating."

"It doesn't?"

"No, that's how come pirates with wooden legs are so unlucky in their pillaging on the seas and such. They're stuck with only three limbs left."

Amy frowned. "I would think they already had the bad luck, to have a leg torn off in the first place. Then having a wooden one would probably slow them down on the stealing of things and that would be why they didn't pillage as well."

It sounded like she was maybe dismissing the power of four. "I'm telling you, it's the three limbs that cause the bad luck."

She hesitated. "We had a three-legged cat once and it seem to get around right good for having a bad-numbered-limb curse."

I glared at her. Hated to do it, but going into battle without loyalty is no way to go about things. "A cat has several lives, so they aren't bothered by things like bad luck."

Amy scratched her head, looking doubtful.

"Listen, Amy. Bad luck sticks around things it can mess with the most. That's people and pigs, mostly."

"I thought a pig was good luck!"

Good Lord, we were wasting time. I had to keep it simple for her. "Amy Lawrence, do you ever eat bacon?"

"Why, yes. I love bacon."

"Of course you do. Everybody does. And a pig isn't raised for nothing but bacon. If you don't call that bad luck, I don't know what you call it. Now four times and spit!"

We clapped hands four times and spit over each other's shoulder. Amy hit my neck, but I didn't begrudge her at all. I wanted to make her feel real good because she was my best friend, and also because I didn't want her running off and leaving me.

"Amy Lawrence, you're about the best partner a thief could have," I told her.

Her eyes clung to a spot just below my ear. "Sorry about your neck."

"Don't worry about that. I moved. Barely touched me. You did just fine."

We crept up the three porch steps (I indicated that we should skip step number two, due to it being October) and squatted down near the open window. Turns out the house wasn't completely dark. I took a look inside and could just make out a sitting room. A low-flamed lamp sat on a table, glowing just enough for the room to look mighty eerie. I settled back into a low position, considering our approach.

A scratching and sniffing noise came from the corner of the porch.

"What's that?" Amy's knees knocked so hard she nearly fell out of her squat.

"Shh! Probably a raccoon."

The sniffing started again and I saw where it came from. A doghouse was tucked in a double shadow of night and porch cover.

"*Charlemagne*," I whispered.

Amy must've thought I'd said a spell because she whimpered and tried to repeat the word.

The hound dog stood and padded out of his house. He seemed to tower miles above us, until I remembered we were squatting.

I stood, pulling Amy up and dug into my pocket for the bacon. I held out a piece, then thought better and tossed all of it toward his bed. The dog followed the bacon, and I caught sight of a familiar ragged cloth sticking out of his house. It was the piece of torn shirt that had been dangling from Charlemagne's mouth back at the cemetery. Billy Pritchard's shirt.

Amy gripped my arm and stood behind me. "What now?" she whispered.

"Quick, reach inside the witch's window and find something!"

She obeyed, while the dog was kept busy with the bacon. We both had our arms stuck in the window and were frantically waving around for something, *anything*, when I felt a hand grab mine.

I screamed, and Amy must've felt the same thing, because I felt her stiffen and slump beside me, having fainted dead away. The mystery hand dropped mine, and I heard footsteps move around the house. Charlemagne approached, thin ropes of drool lining his jaw. He was done with the bacon and looking for something more hearty to eat on.

Something like an eleven-year-old girl.

The back door blasted open and the witch herself stood in the doorway, holding a devil's wand in her hand.

I about peed my pants.

"Hey!" she yelled, raising the evil cursing stick.

"No!" I threw my body over Amy Lawrence, determined to die a brave and valiant death for my best friend. I only wished she were conscious to see me do it.

"Charlie, *down*!"

To my surprise, the Widow was pointing at the dog, not me. And also, the devil's wand wasn't a devil's wand at all. It looked to be a wooden cooking spoon with some kind of dough on it. The dog was lapping at the porch floor where some had flicked off.

"What on earth happened to your friend?"

"Are you gonna curse us?" I had to ask. The wooden spoon might have been a trick. If I recalled, there was some fairy tale about a witch who cooked goodies for unsuspecting fools that passed. Then she would eat the fools and gobble the goodies for dessert. "We taste like pickled liver!" I blurted out. That was the worst thing I'd ever tried, so maybe she wouldn't want to eat us.

Widow Douglas bent down, examining Amy, probably seeing if her arms were fat enough to eat. Lucky for Amy, she's thin as a rail like me.

Amy's eyes fluttered and she moaned, rubbing her head. She sat up and nearly fainted again at the sight of the Widow. "Becky! It's the—"

"Shh! Stop talking nonsense, both of you." Widow Douglas

bent over to peer closely at Amy. "You all right, honey?"

Hmm. She didn't sound like she wanted to eat us, but it was hard to tell for sure. "Ma'am, I think she might have hit her head when she—"

"When you two were trying to steal something from me?" The Widow waited for an answer, not looking too intimidating in a simple blue dress. But what was she doing still dressed in day clothes? Up doing spells, no doubt. She gave me a tight-lipped stare, but then grinned and laughed. "You two come on in and we'll make sure she's okay."

She was crazy all right, but I guess she had us in her clutches. Best not to make any sudden moves. She might set her hound on us.

The Widow lit a few lamps and the house brightened like it was early evening, not nearing midnight. It smelled like baked goods, and despite my lingering fears, I found myself sniffing the air and sighing at the delicious scent. Then I gave myself a good pinch so I'd stay on guard. A cookie-smelling house was just the thing a tricky witch would use to make a child-size thief relax.

"Now, dears," she said with a small firm smile, "we still haven't been properly introduced. You're the Lawrence girl, aren't you?"

"Her name is Amy," I said. "And I'm Becky Thatcher."

"A pleasure to meet you both. I'm Katherine Douglas." The Widow tapped Amy, causing her to let out a small shriek. "Oh my, dear. You're awfully jumpy. Would you girls like something hot to drink? The nights are finally starting to get cool."

Amy looked at me and shook a tiny, fierce *no* with her head, but something hot sounded real good to me. Plus, we could look around while she was fetching the drinks. "Yes, please," I said.

"I'll just go put the kettle on. I got some fresh pie and cookies, too. You girls go on in the sitting room." She disappeared, and I wondered what all a witch kept in her cupboards.

Amy and I stepped into a room with a sofa, three high-backed chairs, and a low center table. Nothing looked too witchy. I wasn't about to relax completely, but being in the Widow's place wasn't nearly as frightening as having Billy Pritchard's blade against my throat. The only sign of disarray was a pile of oddly-bunched cloth curtains on the floor next to a parlor window.

"Poison," Amy hissed, clutching my side and throwing a glance toward the window where Charlemagne was looking in. "Becky, the Widow Witch's sure to slip poison in the drinks and food."

I nodded at the possibility. "She surely might. Hospitality from a witch is always suspicious. She might not, though, and I'd hate to miss out on whatever's making that sweet smell. Besides," I whispered, "if we're gonna be chopped up and stuffed in a witch brew then I reckon I wouldn't mind being dead first. Can you imagine getting chopped up when you're good and alive, Amy? I'd much rather get poisoned with some tea and cookies before that mess got started."

From the awful look on her face and the increased grip from her fingers on my waist, Amy's imagination worked just fine.

"I'll try everything first, okay? If I start to feel poisoned I'll wink three times and run out the front door to die. When the Widow comes to fetch my body, you run out the back door." I gently removed her clawed hand from my side and patted it. "You'll make it out alive."

"What about the dog?" she asked. "The dog'll be out back."

I was a little hurt that she was willing to have me sacrifice myself for her without a hint of protest, but I had long ago realized that while she was the sweetness, I was the moral rock in our friendship. "Then I'll go out back to die," I assured her. "Now, let's just enjoy what might be our last minutes together. Sure is a nice house."

The sofa was covered in flower fabric, everything was clean, and the side tables looked polished. There was a dark wood shelf with delicate plates displayed on it and another shelf filled with books. There were some framed pencil sketches of a pretty young girl sitting under a tree. One larger sketch was of a boy and girl from the back, holding hands and sitting on a river dock. The girl's head was on the boy's shoulder. At the bottom it said *James and his Katie*.

A few black-and-white photographs were scattered on the end tables, all with a man about Daddy's age who had his arm around a pretty young lady. They were dressed up, him in a suit and fancy hat and her in a fur coat.

The Widow came in, setting a tray on the center coffee table and handing me a cup of tea. She passed Amy a cup of tea before settling herself in an armchair and gesturing to the other seats. "Sit down, sit down."

Amy nodded and sat stiffly on the far side of the flowered sofa. I sat in the middle of the sofa, giving Amy a cushion between her and any witchery.

"Baked the pie this afternoon." Pointing to the burnt orange filling, she smiled. "It's pumpkin. Can I cut you a big—"

"No!" I blurted as Sid Sawyer's words sprang to mind. Visions of stolen children's heads crept from my thoughts to my fingers, sending my tea cup rattling on its drip dish. "I, um, well, I believe pumpkin doesn't sit well on my stomach."

Amy set her tea down. "I'll just wait until this cools, ma'am," she whispered, eyeing the distance to the front door.

"Fine, dear. Cookie?"

Amy looked fit to vomit. I grabbed the cookie from the Widow's hand and bit in before I could think about it, ignoring Amy's panicked stare. Oatmeal and walnuts, from the taste of it. A little heavy-handed on the walnuts, but otherwise it tasted pretty good. I chewed the whole thing heartily and had just taken a huge gulp of tea to wash it down, when my mouth exploded in pain.

I clean forgot about winking. In my attempt to make it out the back door to die, I stood and stumbled, cracking my shin on the coffee table. Falling to the floor, I gasped for breath like a fish pulled from the Mississippi.

Sweet baby Jesus in a holy hay barn, I'd been poisoned.

Chapter Eleven

A shovel mistake, a yard full of flames, and a witchy prank

Amy pulled me to my feet and moaned at the sight of my wide eyes and mouth. "I knew it! I knew it!" Looking devastated and properly torn, she searched my eyes, most likely for permission to skeedaddle out of the witch's house and leave me for dead.

I pushed her away, wagging my tongue in the air to ease the burning sensation, which was fading. My heart slowed down when I realized I wasn't dying after all. Waving a hand at Amy, who was halfway to the front door, I found my voice again. "It's just ho-ho-hot," I breathed. "That's all."

The Widow's eyebrows were scrunched together in concern, her head turning back and forth between the two of us. "What in Heaven?"

"Sorry about the fuss," I told her. "We just thought you might see fit to poison us, and when the tea scalded me, I thought maybe . . ." My face felt near as hot as my tongue. "Those are nice photographs you got," I added to be polite.

The Widow laughed a little. "My reputation as a witch is alive and well I see. I don't poison all my guests, you know." She picked up a photograph, tracing the figures within. "We had those taken in 1841 on a trip to Philadelphia. James died shortly after we sat for these pictures."

She said it matter-of-factly, but it was strange to me, looking at her husband's smiling face all full of frozen life. Like staring into the eyes of a ghost.

We had only one family photograph, the one I'd seen Mama holding after I snuck home from the grounded steamboat. She'd hidden it the day after Jon's funeral. Every so often, I'd creep into Mama and Daddy's room looking for it. The only thing I'd found was a box full of handkerchiefs she'd embroidered for Jon.

I looked at the Widow Douglas's photograph for another second before letting my eyes lift to the rest of the room. I felt a little awkward, having accused our host of murder and all, but the Widow didn't seem too upset. Still, it would be best if I could say something else that sounded nice to cancel out the tea mishap. "I like your wall paintings," I told her.

Amy and I were both more calm now that I wasn't poisoned, but she still stuck to my back like a possum baby while I stood and studied landscape paintings covering the room's pale blue walls. The paintings were from different angles and had different trees, boats, and people in them, but they were all of the Mississippi River. A painter's easel and brushes stood in the corner.

"Did you paint all these?" I asked.

Amy touched one of the frames. "They're beautiful."

"Bless you girls, no. I didn't paint them. My husband did. That's him and me in the sketches, there, too." A sad smile lifted her lips and her eyes curved down to meet them. "It'll be nearly twenty years ago this Christmas Eve that he left me."

She'd lived alone for a long time. Well, I couldn't hardly blame her for turning into a witch. Not when someone so close to her went and died and she didn't have anyone else.

"Twenty years ago? Then why are his painting supplies still out?" Amy asked, looking confused.

A strange stirring tickled my chest. I smoothed Jon's overalls. I thought maybe I knew why those things were still left out. Seeing them helped ease the crushed-down feeling, the kind that sometimes came when I missed my brother. Why couldn't Mama be more like the Widow instead of hiding Jon's things away like they were secrets for only her eyes?

"Sorry you had to yell at your dog," I said quickly, before the Widow had to answer Amy's question. "We thought he might eat us."

The Widow smiled. "Charlemagne wouldn't hurt anyone unless he thought they were threatening me or my belongings. He's kind as a kitten otherwise."

The Pritchards stole from the Widow. I remembered the way Charlemagne had bitten the short Pritchard's leg and switched to lunge at Billy as soon as the shovel changed hands. I wondered if the dog could tell the difference between two outlaws committing a real crime and two girls just trying to win a harmless bet. Hoped so.

Widow Douglas walked to the back door, opened it, and called for her dog. "These are friends," she told him. Charlemagne bumped her hip and padded straight to me. Laying his head against my thigh, he lifted his big hound-dog eyes and blinked a few times.

"He's sweet on you, Becky!" Amy said, clearly astonished. "That hound doesn't have the devil in him at all, does he?"

The Widow grinned and scratched the dog's ears. "He's a good boy. Sometimes I think Charlie's in touch with the souls of those we lost. He always seems to sense when I'm missing my Jimmy." She scratched again, getting a low grunt of pleasure from the dog. "But most likely he's not sweet on Becky, here. Most likely he's sweet on that bacon you threw him." She winked. "I was watching you girls from the kitchen window."

She poured more tea for me while Amy took a hesitant first sip from her cup.

"Becky, I hear your daddy is involved in investigating something that happened last week. A deputy stopped by yesterday, asking me a few questions."

I shifted uncomfortably. "Oh?"

The Widow kneaded her hands. "It was the strangest thing. He asked me where I'd been when that poor dead man was grave robbed. Have you girls heard anything about that?"

Amy squeezed my hand hard. Not trusting my voice, I nodded and reached for another cookie to munch on.

A deep wrinkle formed between her eyes. "Well, I imagine most of the town knows. I told the deputy I was right here, but then he hauled two garden tools onto my porch and demanded to know why the paint seemed less faded on my shovel than on the hoe lying in the side yard." She shook her head. "Said that if I couldn't explain myself properly, there would be consequences."

For a second I was glad I didn't have the hot drink in my mouth, because I would have sprayed it all over her nice house or maybe even into Charlemagne's face. That kind of thing can turn a dog against you, especially when you're clean outta bacon. "What kind of consequences?" I asked, my voice squeaking.

"He just said if things weren't resolved in the Law's eyes, I could expect a trial to take place next week."

Good Lord, a trial next week? "What did you say?" I asked, picturing the Widow locked up, pointing crooked, cursing fingers toward my house.

"Not much. I agreed that it didn't look like my shovel. Mine's got a piece missing near the base where Charlemagne used to chew it as a puppy. I don't even know where he found that other shovel and he wouldn't tell me. Your daddy say anything to you about all this?"

Unable to look her in the eye, I studied the layer of dirt under my fingernails. Mama used to scold me for letting it build up like that. "I reckon he mentioned it, ma'am. It's just a misunderstanding. They found a red-tipped shovel over by the graveyard, and it looked like a pretty big dog had been around there too . . . so . . ." I gulped at the air like I was trying to catch butterflies, hoping the words to make everything okay would find their way into my mouth.

My mistake smacked me on the head like a blunt shovel tip. The sheriff would likely send someone to the Bumpners' shed, based on what I'd said to Daddy. And to a deputy who hadn't gotten to know the Widow like Amy and I had, who only had paint and garden tools to guide his suspicions, it might just seem like the Widow had stolen the Bumpners' shovel to cover her guilty witch hide. Instead of helping to prove the Widow innocent, I may have accidentally provided evidence to stick her in jail.

The Widow narrowed her eyes at my silence, and Amy widened hers.

I didn't have to be a smarty-pants to know one was thinking, *Well, looks like I'm gonna have to witch these two after all,* and the other was thinking, *Open your dang trap and say something better!*

But the Widow's face settled into a grimace and she let out a heavy sigh. "Well, that's just ridiculous. I didn't do a thing, and dogs don't dig up graves."

"Not with shovels, anyway," Amy muttered.

I gave her a little foot stomp for that unhelpful business.

"That's right, dear. Oh, and you girls can call me Miss Katie, if you'd like." She stood and fiddled with a photograph. "Amy, I was awfully sorry to hear about your mama, sweetheart. I would have said something sooner, but I keep to myself, as I'm sure you all have noticed. Can't seem to get the energy to be around anyone since James died."

All of a sudden, I felt real bad about trying to steal from her. "Mrs. Douglas, there might be some boys coming over to your house in a little while. You see . . ." I trailed off, trying to think of a delicate way to put the whole betting scheme.

"Don't worry," she said. "I'll have something special ready

for them." She stood and walked over to what I'd thought was a pile of curtains on the floor. Instead, it turned out to be a set of sheets that she had rigged to a string of barely visible fishing line. "See this? That nice river pilot helped me. He figured it would be enough to startle anybody ready to be startled."

That Sam Clemens. Between telling me about the Widow's open window and helping her with a prank, he'd been playing both sides of the witchy bet. Part of me resented Sam's interference, and another part was pleased that a full-grown man was still capable of mischief. It was just the type of thing Jon might've done if he'd lived to be full grown.

With one mighty yank of her hand, the sheets sprang off the Widow's floor and shot across the room, straight past the window. She let out a hoot. "What do you think?"

Flying through the air, the cloth did a mighty good imitation of haunting figures. I stood and clapped in appreciation, trying to memorize the design. It was a neat trick, that was certain.

The Widow sure seemed pleased. She returned the sheets to the floor and yanked again, cackling at the makeshift spirits. She might not have been an evil kind of witch, but she sure seemed to enjoy a ghostly trick.

"It's just a back-up plan, of course. I wrung the necks of two chickens earlier today. Figured I'd hang the hens upside down in the doorway." She winked at me. "You know the old saying?"

"Hey!" I said. "That's right!"

Amy wrinkled her nose. "What's right?"

I cleared my throat and recited:

"Feet over head, chicken in a door,
Lay down dead if you cross my floor,
Boy-as-hen, you'll hang till you've died,
No good'll come if you come inside."

Amy stood and smiled. "Oh! Joe Harper told me that one when we went walking. He said he and Sid were hiding a stash of rotten eggs in the shed last year, since they were fixing to go egging someone that night. Anyway, they didn't want anybody searching the shed, so they strung up a dead chicken. Didn't work. Tom found the eggs, of course, and told Aunt Polly." She looked at me, probably expecting to share a look of loathing for Tom Sawyer.

Instead, I frowned. "Amy Lawrence, when did you go walking with Joe Harper?"

Amy blushed, but the Widow laughed and nodded. "My Jimmy was as superstitious as those boys you run around with. I don't know where they hear that foolishness, but it sticks with them well into their manhood."

A muffled thump hit the front of the house. I turned and scanned the opening between the curtains on the window, seeing nothing.

"You girls win your bet and then come back and visit with me." The Widow walked to a writing desk in the corner of the room and took a piece of paper from a drawer. "You can take my stationery for evidence. James got it for me years ago so I could write poetry. You might say I write all my spells on it." She squeezed my shoulder and gave me the paper. It said *Katherine Douglas* along the bottom.

I was so surprised, I didn't even think of catching warts from her spell paper, though the next time I washed, I would most likely check to make sure none had sprouted.

The Widow's face flushed a little, probably from the tea. "So, do you think you might come visit again?"

Amy kicked me and mouthed the words *witch trap*, shifting her eyes to the Widow with a few jabby and pointed glances that made her look cross-eyed.

I ignored her and put the paper into my overall bib. "We'd be happy to." If Jon could be acquaintances with spirit men who were on speaking terms with folks from the Other Side, I reckoned we could be acquainted with a non-evil-doing witch.

Another thump landed. This time I decided to investigate. Stepping through the parlor, I lifted my feet over Charlemagne, who had settled himself on the floor, and moved the curtain aside on the center window. "What's that?" Four sticks, each about two feet long, were ablaze on the front lawn. At first I thought it was supposed to be a cross, but as the flames dimmed to a steady glow, I realized what I was looking at.

Amy and the Widow hurried to my side.

"Fire! Good Lord, is that . . . is that the letter *W*?" The Widow Douglas put a hand to her chest. "Someone put a burning *W* on my lawn?" Her eyes filled with fear. "I wasn't expecting something like burning my lawn. Good Lord, is my house going to catch fire?"

"Witch!" cried Amy. "It's a *W* for witch!"

It took everything I had not to slap Amy Lawrence upside the head.

I did have to admire the boys' cleverness. It was a beauty of a distraction. An unattended Widow was certain to hear the thumping and come flying out onto her front porch, leaving the back open for pillaging.

"Your house'll be fine. Ma'am, do you have any flour?"

She pointed to the kitchen door. "Pantry's in there. Got a twenty-pound sack on the first shelf. Hasn't been opened."

I grabbed the sack with some difficulty and headed out the front door. "Amy, look out the back. No doubt they're running around right now. Get those chickens up!" I hurried out the door and struggled down the steps with the bag.

Up close, I could see that the fire wasn't too bad. Sid and Joe had poured sand all around the cloth-banded and oiled sticks, so the fire couldn't go anywhere. I guess that's what Sid meant by fetching sand. Maybe those two boys weren't so dumb after all.

A shout down the road made my head shoot up. In the dark I couldn't be certain, but I could have sworn I saw a boy standing at the corner of the next block. It almost looked like . . . Tom Sawyer? Cursing, I slit the bag open with my pocket knife and poured a steady stream of flour over the *W* until all I could see was a white cloud.

Before the flour dust cleared enough to get a proper look at the spy, I heard two bloody screams from behind the house.

Sid and Joe sprinted around the corner and jumped the Widow's fence.

I met the Widow and Amy on the front porch, all three of us laughing like the best of friends. "You got the fire out," the Widow said. "Thank you, Becky."

"Yes, ma'am. It'll leave an awful mark, though." I looked

toward the Sawyer house. It was dark and silent. "I must have inhaled some smoke or flour dust, because I could have sworn I saw Tom Sawyer watching me stand over those flames. But I reckon he'd wake the whole town if he thought he could get me in trouble. Must've been my imagination."

"We can't have you getting in trouble, or I won't have anyone to visit." The Widow grinned just the tiniest bit. "Fetch that shovel from under my porch for me before you go. I have a mind to do some midnight gardening." She nodded to herself, scanning her front yard.

Good Lord, the Widow sure was friendly, but she was also loony as a waterbird. "What, ma'am?"

"Never you mind. And you call me Mrs. Douglas, if you can't call me Katie."

I fetched her the shovel, then stood twiddling my thumbs for a good minute while the Widow Douglas watched the moon, probably doing some kind of silent chant to get its powers into her. I realized she most likely had some spell-casting to do over her autumn herbs. The more I thought about it, midnight gardening made perfect sense. "Mrs. Douglas, do you mind if we get going? We got to meet up with the boys." I tapped my overall pocket and smiled. "Thank you for the paper."

"Of course, dear. Like I was telling Amy, I haven't had this much company since I don't remember when." She patted our hands, just like a normal, non-witchy grandmother would do.

It was so nice that it nearly broke my heart to know that my shovel-shuffling actions might get her arrested for a crime she didn't commit.

While Amy and I made our way to the schoolhouse, I

realized I needed a new plan. Jon always said that plans had more interesting possibilities when there was money involved. If five dollars and my years of experience making mischief weren't enough to buy some sort of miracle to clear the Widow's name, not only would she be shut in jail, but I'd be doomed to confession and punishment to save her.

As the schoolhouse roof came into view, I reasoned that the very best thing to do for both my own freedom and the Widow's was to fetch the winnings. I'd work on the rest when the sun came up. The way I figured, no other messes were likely to turn up before then.

I sure hoped my figuring was right.

Chapter Twelve

Trouble in the schoolhouse

Sid and Joe sat inside the schoolhouse like they were waiting for class to start, except they had a lantern lit and Joe was coughing from the tobacco he was attempting to smoke. Amy and I paused outside and listened at the window they had cracked open on the river side of the building.

"Put that out, Joe," Sid was scolding. "Where'd you find it anyway?"

"Back of the schoolhouse, same place we found that clump last time. Someone dropped a whole rolled cigarette. It's the expensive kind—empty tobacco tin was there too." He hacked and hacked. "There's no way Davy Fry's daddy smokes Reed's brand. Somebody else has got to be smoking back there. Somebody with money."

"Put it out! You're making me even more nervous than I already am."

"I'm trying to calm *my* nerves, but it doesn't seem to be helping. Sid, you reckon the Widow Witch got a hold of the girls?" Joe's voice shook as he flicked the cigarette out the window, grazing Amy's arm with the lit side.

Before she could make a sound, I stamped on the cigarette, lifted the sill another foot, and poked my head in. "Hello, you smelly catfish!"

They both jumped near out of their skins when we hauled ourselves into the school. Seeing them so startled was almost as fun as collecting our money would be.

"You're alive!" shouted Joe, a look of wild wonder filling his face. He stood and rushed over to us, breathing out like he'd been saving up air for a week. Then, just as suddenly as he'd started toward us, he stopped short and shoved both hands into his pockets, rocking back on his heels. "You're alive," he repeated in a quieter voice. He half-grinned, then frowned and shrugged his shoulders. "I guess that's good."

"Thank the Lord," said Sid, looking considerably relieved. "I thought I was gonna have to tell your daddies we got you killed."

"Where are the others?"

Joe laughed. "They backed out. Heard that the Widow Witch was going to the graveyard to fetch that body she tried to dig up. Heard she'd be up all night long, messing with it."

Sid squirmed in his chair.

"And how'd they hear that?" I asked.

With a wicked smile, Joe tilted his head at Sid. "He told 'em." His lips fell and twisted to one side. "We didn't know she'd really be working on something like that."

It was my turn to smile. "Sounds to me like you two nearly got stuck in a stew pot yourselves. What happened to you?"

Amy and I hadn't discussed what happened at the Widow's house, but her eyes twinkled. "I think they might've caught sight of the Widow Witch herself, chanting and making an evil brew on her stovetop. Might have seen a ghost, too."

"Hoo!" Joe's eyebrows shot up and he gripped Sid by the arm. "That's it! That's just what Sid and I saw!"

Sid's eyes narrowed and his gaze drifted down to my hands. "I'll be a pot-bellied pig in britches, what's that?" He snatched the paper. "Did you two get in there?"

"That's right. And we did it without setting fire to anything. Pay up, gentlemen."

Joe scowled at the floor. "Money's with Petey Todd," he said. "We'll have to discuss things in the morning."

Amy poked Joe right in the shoulder. "There'll be no discussing, Joe Harper. We earned that money. Let's go get it. Now."

A blush crept to Joe's cheeks. It must've been a bad one 'cause you could tell how red he was even in the dim lamplight. "Petey's family is all in bed, and I'm not trying to break into any more houses tonight." He blew out the lamp.

Well, shoot. I needed that light to get Jon's marbles back. "Wait! Bring a match or something over to Dob-head's desk. Is there a ruler somewhere?"

Amy found a ruler in the small supply cabinet and handed it to me while Sid lit a match and held it by our teacher's desk. I wedged my knife tip in the bottom desk drawer and yanked back. It budged just enough to slip the ruler into the empty space before Sid cursed and the match died. He lit another and I pried the drawer open just enough to snatch the marbles.

Right as I did, an annoyed yell came from somewhere beyond the far side of the schoolhouse—the side opposite our open window. I blew out the second match.

"Who's that?" asked Joe, earning three smacks upside the head.

"Shh," I whispered. "Let's get outta here."

It's a good thing the four of us were experienced sneaker-outers. We barely made a sound slipping out the window and sliding it down. We weren't twenty yards away, near the creek, when a dim light went on inside the schoolhouse. The gravelly sound of distant mumbling drifted toward us on a night breeze.

"Who's that?" Joe whispered again, guarding his head just in case.

"Don't know," said Sid. "Nobody should have business around here this time of night."

"Maybe it's Dobbins with a woman," said Joe.

We all stared at him for about three seconds before collapsing on the ground with laughter. I tried hard to stay quiet, but a couple of snorts came out.

A massive groan of pain from the school halted our hee-hawing. A sharp, low-pitched cry followed, then more squawking and grunting. A few choice swear words rang out our way, nagging at me for a reason I couldn't quite get a fix on. After a moment of quiet, there was a noise that almost sounded like a man sobbing.

"We better get going," Sid said. "Whoever's in there and whatever they're up to, it's no business of ours."

Amy and I agreed. Though I knew from books and stories and such that marauders would never get within a mile of a schoolhouse other than to leave threatening notes (they're more partial to taverns and graveyards and places worth robbing), the Pritchard brothers crept into my mind. Daddy had said there was no use getting people riled up for no reason and there was no guarantee that the Pritchards were in town, but it was a struggle not to tell the boys about the outlaws' plans to return to St. Petersburg.

We reached the Sawyer place and were surprised to see a light shining from a small second floor window.

Joe gave a low whistle. "What's a light doing on at your house? It must be near one o'clock in the morning."

Maybe it was the moonlight, but Sid's face seemed to be turning a sick shade of yellow-green. "That's Tom's room," he said.

"Kiss my grits," I swore. "That brother of yours has done it again." I hit Sid's shoulder.

Joe spit on the ground. "How'd he find out, that sneak!" Though he sounded mad, I could tell Joe was as worried as the rest of us.

"I thought I saw Tom when I was putting out your flames," I told Sid. "Probably told Aunt Polly that I tried to set Mrs. Douglas's house on fire."

"Who's Mrs. Douglas?" Joe asked. His face wrinkled up like when Dobbins asked him a math question.

"You can go to jail for doing something like that!" Amy cried.

And the Widow might go to jail for grave robbing, I thought. *Maybe we'll be stuck in the same cell.*

Sid paced back and forth, wagging his head like he was trying to shake off a skitter. "But Tom couldn't have . . . He didn't know . . ." His jaw flapped up and down a few times as he stared my way, but he didn't say any more. He didn't need to.

"I reckon he's already told Aunt Polly some version of what he saw," I said. "Amy, you best get home. Boys, you do the same."

After Sid and Joe left us, Amy lunged at me, squishing me in a hard embrace. She squeezed me so tight I felt her rabbit-quick heartbeat against my chest. "What are you gonna do?"

I was angry and scared and having trouble thinking of an answer to her question. "Don't you worry, Amy. Just know that you can have all the winnings if you don't see me for a while. I'm giving you my half."

"What? Becky, what are you going to do?"

I ran down the road toward my house before either of us could start crying. Nobody would believe me over that goody-goody Tom Sawyer and if I went to jail, there wouldn't be anybody left to save the Widow. And Daddy would never get over the shame if the sheriff stuck me behind bars. There was only one thing to do.

I had to get back home and gather some supplies. I wasn't sure where to hide out, but I needed to run far enough to get away from the trouble that'd latched onto me like a river leech. Maybe I could think of a solution once I got some distance. I'd need a big enough lie to cover up all the other lies that'd been told.

My marble sack jiggled as I walked, and I took comfort in the fact that Jon would see running away as an adventure. So would Sam Clemens, probably. Come to think about it, Sam's steamboat might just make the perfect hideout spot while I determined my next move.

No lights were on at my house, so I assumed Aunt Polly was waiting until morning to tell my daddy the news. A tall ladder lay in the backyard from where Daddy had hired someone to look at the chimney before winter set in. Hauling the ladder over to my bedroom window and climbing the rungs, I stewed like a potful of meat and potatoes, wondering when Sid and Joe's flaming wooden letter would be traced back to me. The sooner I put together a provision sack and headed back outside, the more time I'd have to think up a plan.

But all the giddy energy gushing through my body retreated at the sight of my bed. Despite my intention to run off, my legs resisted the idea of gallivanting into the night and my feet led me to the edge of my soft comforter and pillow.

Don't you lay down, I told myself.

Aw, just for a minute, I argued back.

I'm not foolin', you stay awake!

But instead, my stubborn body went ahead and fell asleep.

Chapter Thirteen

Steamboat blues

When I woke, it was still dark, but just barely. The stars were all but winked out and a low glow was trying to bust over the horizon. Listening hard, I didn't hear any sign of activity in the house, not even a mama snore. With a peek outside, I saw that my ladder had fallen to the ground. Miss Ada's cabin was dark. Today was Sunday, her day off, and it looked like she was still sleeping. With considerable relief, I shook the prickles from my cramped muscles. It was time to run away before people started stirring and getting ready for church. And before I could ponder the sort of punishment I'd be getting if Daddy caught me sneaking out again.

A memory struck while I tiptoed downstairs for supplies. All those times Jon had taken a licking or missed supper as punishment, Mama had always gone to him after Daddy was done being the Judge. I would watch her walk up the stairs, her apron bulging with a roll or cookie, and hear her open Jon's door. She would ask, *What am I gonna do with you, Jon Thatcher?* Somehow, the question always sounded exactly like she was saying *I love you.* My eyes got itchy at that thought. Mama hadn't said any kind of *I love you* to me in quite awhile.

Blinking real good before any troublesome tears could fall, I made a quick stop in the kitchen and took off with four left-over biscuits, a fried chicken leg, my bag of marbles, a straw hat, and no shoes. The sweet grass of the backyard felt cold as a glass of iced tea. It was a chilly October morning, that was for sure. My toes dug into the ground, curling up for warmth and finding only squishy ground. A light rain must've fallen after I got home.

I did a few jumps and squats to warm up. Cow plop, this running away wasn't much fun so far. I looked back at the fallen ladder and wondered whether I should try telling the truth to set me and the Widow Douglas free, but I slapped my own cheek to knock that nonsense outta my head. In my experience, adults seldom took to hearing a child's truth, least not without a heap of doubt or a switch involved afterward.

I made my way to the woods on the north side of town and cut across the stream at a low point. I followed the water, feeling moss on the trees as I went. The birds weren't awake yet, but the earth sure was. The moist greens and browns, the ferns and critters and slugs. They all seemed to vibrate with the happiness of being clean. It was in the drip-drips and drip-drops that still fell from the branches and dampened my lashes. Everything looked fresh and new.

I ignored the scratch of twiggy ground cover and rolled my

pant legs up, bounding through the bushes and ferns, fighting hard not to let the bursting in my chest come out as a whoop of freedom. In the days since Jon died, whenever I had started feeling too heavy, I put on his clothes and went running, running, running. If I found a thick enough patch of woods, it was almost like those leaves were him, slapping my side and tearing up the brush right beside me. Alive again.

I found my way to the riverbank.

"Hello, Miss Issippi," I said. "You're looking awful pretty this morning, with that fog coming off your water. You're going your way and I'm going mine." I tipped my hat, but the Miss ignored me. I didn't mind a bit, though. I liked the river real well.

I followed a narrow fisherman's trail up-current until I got to the grounded steamer. Dipping my foot into the river, I realized that the dirt, however chilly, was mighty tolerable compared to the temperature of the water that early in the morning.

The steamer was right against the shore, same way it was the night Tom Sawyer first told on me. And here I was, back again because he had snitched to Aunt Polly about what he thought I'd done. And as soon as light made it proper, he'd be telling the rest of the world. Maybe he'd make an announcement at church. I hated to think of Mrs. Sprague's disappointed face.

At least the Mississippi didn't care. It was so big and full of life, but it still didn't mind letting us do our business in and around it. Can't think of a person in the world with that kind of meekness and bigness all at once. Maybe Jesus was that way. That's why there are so many rivers in the Bible and why He was always letting people wash His feet with river water. I stared at the Miss, watching the first bit of sunlight make flashes on the water. I wondered if Jon up in Heaven could see those flashes, if he'd met Jesus at all, and if he'd put in a good word for me.

No gangplank was down, so I scanned the side of the boat for dangling ropes. Seeing none, I switched my gaze to the shoreline and quickly found a route. I scooted up a tree that had an overhanging branch and dropped onto the silent boat, making my way to a load of ropes and boxes stacked against the railing. From that spot I'd be close to cover in case someone came aboard, but I could still look far down the waterway. Daddy said the Mississippi went all the way to the ocean.

Just imagine, Jon. The ocean.

I took the leather bag from my bib pocket and searched for the right marble to hold while I thought of my brother. Blue? The ocean already had so much blue.

The tiger's-eye one. It was brown and yellow and shiny. I decided Jon would like that, me taking a tiger to the ocean for him. I imagined standing right where I was, tucked against the side boards with a whole world waiting to be discovered and explored somewhere in all that water.

"Hey!"

My body jerked in surprise and I nearly fell over the railing as Sam Clemens came up behind me carrying two steaming mugs. "Coffee?"

Sam didn't look near as scruffy as me with his black pants, unwrinkled white shirt, and black suspenders, but his hair was good and messy. It stuck up all over the place, like maybe it'd gotten in a fight with his pillow the night before. He stepped alongside me and held out one of the cups.

I didn't drink coffee any more than the next eleven-year-old girl, but it looked good enough to ignore that fact. Watching what Sam did, I blew on my drink and took a mouthful, noting how it smelled better than it tasted. Swishing around the slightly sour flavor, I wondered when people grew up enough to start preferring bitterness to sweetness.

Sam drank, smacking his lips after each gulp. "Mind telling me what you're doing here?" He didn't say it mean, like some adults. In fact, he seemed almost happy for the company, the way he had a hot drink ready for me and was settling down on the boxes like he was expecting to have a friendly chat.

Considering his question, I decided that Sam Clemens might be the one adult I could tell the truth to. I cleared my throat. "I'm running away," I told him, straightening my shoulders so Sam would know I was serious.

He took another sip of coffee and nodded. "This doesn't have to do with Tom Sawyer coming into the house late last night and waking Aunt Polly, does it?"

I smacked my forehead. "He woke her up?"

He grinned. "I heard doors open a few times last night. I figured Sid would stick to using windows if he was leaving at night, so I knew it had to be Tom. Plus, he was making extra noise by pacing back and forth. Seems he was trying to figure out whether to wake her or not."

"And he did, that lowdown slug!"

"No, Aunt Polly woke up on her own from Tom's feet thumping all over the place. Says she's a light sleeper with Sid sneaking out so much. Anyhow, Tom said that Sid wasn't in his bed. Then he claimed he saw you down by the Widow

Douglas's, setting fire to something." He shook his head, laughing. "I was up by then, so we all went to Sid's room."

"And?"

"And he looked to be sleeping like a baby. Aunt Polly didn't seem to notice the muddy footprints on the floor, so I didn't feel the need to point them out."

I sighed in relief. At least Sid was safe. "What then? Did everyone go back to sleep?"

"I wish that had been the case. Tom was considerably puzzled. Puzzled enough that he wanted to drag Aunt Polly down the road to make sure nobody's front lawn was on fire."

I sucked in a breath. "And?"

He winked. "I offered to go instead. Walked over and didn't see a thing. Where he claimed to see you setting a fire, there was a nice new garden circle dug up. Good clump of herbs growing in it too."

"There was?" Mrs. Douglas had saved my hide. "I mean, of course there was. It's not like anyone would be setting fire to the Widow's yard. What happened then?"

"If you'll believe it, Tom got a talking-to and was sent to bed with a promise of no breakfast before church."

So I wouldn't be getting the switch after all, at least not for something I didn't do. Still, there was the matter of the grave robbing and a certain set of outlaws I'd seen and heard. But I didn't want to think about the Pritchards or the Widow or anybody. I shook my head to rid it of all my thoughts and realized Sam was still talking.

". . . I'd had enough nonsense, so I came to sleep on my

boat." Taking a few deep breaths, he looked far down the Miss. "I love this river."

"I do too."

He set his cup on the railing and turned to me, eyes wide and curious. "Why's that?"

"Is that a trick question?"

He laughed. "No, no. I'd genuinely like to know."

"Okay, then." I'd given the matter some thought, having spent plenty of time around the water since moving to St. Petersburg. "The Mississippi's always moving somewhere and keeps to herself, but she still lets you in for a swim and a fish now and then. She lets you skip stones and spit cherry pits far into her, which is nice if you think about it."

"Nice?"

"Sure, it's nice! It'd be like if someone as big as Daddy took to letting ants have picnics on his belly whenever they felt like it. See," I said. "Look at it all."

The morning fog was starting to burn off. Boats dotted the waterway, looking like cows grazing on the river's surface. A thin line of smoke rose in the air right where the river bent beyond our view, indicating a steamboat heading south. Distant shouting came from upriver at the St. Petersburg dock, and a tiny splash sounded just below us when some critter took to the water. The Mississippi and her banks were alive, there was no doubt of that.

"And she's big enough that she probably can't tell the difference between a turtle or a child or a grown-up jumping in," I said. I thought of how Jon never, not once, stepped lightly into the town pond back in Riley. How he always took flying leaps with the biggest, wildest smile on his face, even if you dared him on the coldest day of winter.

I wanted to be just like that, taking leaps into life instead of dipping one toe in at a time.

I inhaled and held the river air inside me. "When you're on this river, you can stay any age and be whoever you want. The Mississippi lets you make any kind of splash you need to, and she doesn't judge you for it one bit. She doesn't ask you to change."

Sam nodded slowly, giving the Miss a soft smile. "That's true." He reached for his cup, frowning at its emptiness. "How long you planning on staying a runaway, if you don't mind my asking?"

I shrugged.

"A steamboat isn't the best place for running away. There's an island upriver that would make a nice spot. Come to think of it, though, there's not much reason for you to be running off anymore, is there?"

"Guess not," I said. Now that I wasn't going to jail, I could go back home to figure out how to save the Widow Douglas without getting punished. "If I stay out any longer, people might start thinking I fell in the river and drowned. Miss Ada would be awful sad at my funeral. Come to think of it, not too many people get to see their own funeral. Might be worth an extra couple of days."

His eyes twinkled. "Isn't that an idea? Visiting your own funeral." He took out his notebook and jotted something down. "So just Miss Ada would be sad, you think?"

"Amy Lawrence would be considerable sad too," I allowed, studying my bare feet. *She might think the Pritchards snatched me*. Selfishly, I wondered once again if Mama would snap out of her silence if she thought marauders had taken my life.

"They'd be scouring these shorelines with dogs," Sam said. "Might think those Pritchards got you."

My head whipped up, but he seemed to be joking instead of reading my mind. Like Daddy and the sheriff, he thought the Pritchards had moved on. The mention of dogs reminded me of something. *The Widow's dog ripped a piece of Billy Pritchard's shirt*. A flicker of an idea formed.

I tried to sound casual. "Speaking of dogs, do you reckon Charlemagne could pick up on a scent?"

"That's what hound dogs tend to do, if I understand the way of things. By the way, did you ever go over there and get acquainted with the Widow?"

I shifted side to side, then twisted my legs. That coffee had hit my bladder. "You might say that. She's not a *bad* witch, you know."

"Well, I can't say for certain, but you're probably right." He plucked his cup from the railing, eyed it like he was hoping it would fill itself, and walked toward the stairwell.

It occurred to me that Sam Clemens didn't have a Miss Ada or a wife on the steamboat to fetch him more. Then again, having people around was no guarantee that they'd make good company. For a moment, I wondered if it got as lonely on the river as it had been in our house. Something else struck me. "Why'd you help set up those ghosty sheets that flew around the room?"

Sam grinned at the river. "Well, fishing line's mighty tricky for an older woman's hands. Did she make the oatmeal cookies?

Those are real nice." He turned back to the stairs and held out a hand of farewell. "I've got some shipping paperwork to get settled, so go on home after you finish your coffee. And for the love of women and whiskey, don't let Tom Sawyer see you sneaking back to your house." With that, he walked down the stairs to the steamboat's lower level.

I stared downriver while the sun finished rising. The light was an aching kind of beautiful. Soft streaks of pink-red and orange-red and yellow-orange crept over the horizon and seemed to hold all the world's memories, both good and bad.

Jon was in that sunrise.

I felt his warmth, and for some reason my mind drifted to the opposite coldness of Mama. I suspected that, for her, the thought of Jon was still a place of darkness.

I remembered the first days and weeks after Jon passed, where I couldn't see anything but his death. It flowed inside me. Burned through me until I couldn't breathe, let alone talk.

There are certain people that are so much a part of you, that are so loved, that they shine up your insides just by being around. They fill in all your parts that feel empty and when they leave the world, you don't know how to be without them. You just feel the wind blowing through all those holes they left behind on the way up to Heaven.

And you can't die with that person, but you can change yourself while you figure out how in the world you're gonna replace all the missing pieces inside you. Miss Ada smiled at me more. Daddy didn't joke as much, but he didn't get upset as often either. I wondered if Jon's death was making a difference in me, too. I pinched my knees and legs, then let my fingers drift up to my face, feeling for change. The outside of me felt the same for now.

But Mama had changed into a living ghost. She couldn't get past the cold and dark to see that part of Jon was still here. In overalls and trees and cherry pits. In the sunrise and the water.

"My brother is gone forever to my mama," I whispered to the river. "And she's just about gone forever from me, too." I leaned over the rail, waiting for tears to fall so I could leave my frustration and heartache in the water. So the Mississippi would take those things far, far away.

But no tears came. I closed my eyes, sank into the pile of ropes, and prayed hard. I squeezed everything in me that could be squeezed and begged for Mama to get better and to stop ignoring all the life around her. I pleaded and shouted at God in my head, because I wanted to be heard so badly.

But you can't beg God for things.

God likes poor people and sad people and hurt people, but not beggars. Miss Ada told me that long ago. So instead of saying he'd fix my mama, God hit me over the head with a truth that felt like a blow from a frying pan.

I hadn't run to this steamboat to determine my next move. I'd run away to avoid taking any action at all, and, to boot, I'd abandoned the people who needed my help. For a long minute I wondered why that notion seemed so familiar. When the truth came, it was a painful kind of light, like staring straight into the sun.

I was acting just like Mama.

When I opened my eyes, the path to responsibility and redemption was clear. It would only require a small amount of mischief on my part. Redemption mischief. Hardly any trouble at all.

Chapter Fourteen

———◆———

**Hunting down evidence that might free
an otherwise condemned Widow from
blame for the disturbing indiscretion
of digging up Amos Mutton**

Not caring to run into folks, I crept south along the
Miss. Every time I heard a shout along the river I ducked
and cringed, certain they'd started dragging for my body. With
a watchful eye, I passed the town and loading docks, going as
far as the sawmill before taking a rest and fixing the plan in my
mind. I could hardly believe it when I saw the sun was already
straight above me. Running home, I cursed myself for not paying better attention to the time. Then I cursed time, too, for
not being easier to pay attention to.

Without too much effort or noise, I scooted the fallen
ladder against the window of my room and climbed inside.
There, I weighed both the possibility of the Pritchards stashing their Trittsville load somewhere in St. Petersburg and the
odds of them using the cave Billy'd mentioned at the cemetery to do the stashing. When I was done thinking over my

"taking responsibility" plan, I awaited certain punishment for not being around when Daddy left for Sunday services.

But Daddy never came upstairs, not even when I stomped around a little to let him know that I was inside the house like a good child would be, so I slipped downstairs at two o'clock dressed in a fresh fishskin. I found him at the dining table, surrounded by papers. Even though it was her day off, Miss Ada had set two spots with forks and lemonade for lunch.

"You look busy," I said, giving Daddy a peck on the cheek. "Maybe I'll just go eat in the kitchen, you having all this work for company."

Miss Ada served me some green beans and patted me on the head. "Now Miss Becky, don't you sass your daddy. He's been at the office working nonstop. Didn't even come home last night or get to church this morning. And your mama been sick all day." She grinned at me, but her lips looked stiff and her eyes were just a little too narrow to be friendly, like she knew I'd been up to something. She surveyed the table. "Forgot the pecan pie."

"Pecan pie sounds delicious," I called to Miss Ada's retreating hips. Luck had finally lit upon me like a thirsty skitter! Daddy hadn't noticed a thing about me being gone. I settled into my gravy-soaked chicken, prepared to enjoy the meal.

Daddy stood and tugged on his disappearing hairline before sighing and stretching his arms out like a weary giant. "Becky, would you mind looking in on the Widow Douglas's dog later today?" He yawned and sat back down.

Hmm. Now what on earth could Daddy be getting at with a question like that? "What for, Daddy?" I kept my head down in a heaping plate of chicken and biscuits smothered in white gravy. "That hound'll eat me up as soon as lick me."

Daddy finished a piece of chicken and cleared his throat. "Mrs. Douglas has to come in for more questioning about that body being dug up." He shook his head. "If the deputy is right about his suspicions, we may have underestimated her. And if some of the folks don't take a liking to her answers, then she's liable to be spending the evening with us. That's why she asked that you check on her dog."

Well, shoot. Ladling extra gravy onto my biscuits, I had a hard time keeping my hand steady. "What do you mean, underestimated her?"

Daddy looked me in the eyes. "I wouldn't have believed it myself, but the deputy thinks she's trying to cover up what she did. He and the sheriff suspect she stole the Bumpners' shovel to hide the fact that hers was found at the gravesite. If that's the case, she'll be formally charged this evening." He picked up a biscuit and started buttering.

My spoon plopped right in the gravy, slinging a mess of white sauce between my eyes. "They think the Widow stole the Bumpners' shovel?" I asked, wiping the splatter off my face.

Daddy ignored my question, dropping the biscuit back to his plate. "And the funny thing is that we still don't have a motive for why anyone would dig up Amos Mutton in the first place. Something's not adding up."

Miss Ada swept back in the room and placed the pie between me and Daddy.

"She's being very civil about the whole thing," Daddy continued. "Maybe they won't make her spend the night. It's a

Sunday, after all, and none of us should even be working. Maybe we'll just have the deputy keep watch at the Widow's place to make sure she doesn't take off."

"She wouldn't take off anywhere," I insisted, spraying chicken skin on the tablecloth. "Why, she just put in a new flower bed yesterday. People don't do that and then run off!"

"Calm down, Becky." With two fingers rubbing next to his eyes, Daddy had the look of a man with an awful headache. "Based on word from some people living between Trittsville and here, the Law's now thinking the Pritchards could be hitting St. Petersburg any minute, so you just settle yourself down and stay put. And to think, these fools are more worried about having me lock up an old woman," he mumbled, throwing his napkin on the table. "I don't have much control over anything in my life right now, Becky, but you're my daughter and I'd like you to say, '*Yes, sir, I'll look in on the dog and stay close to home*' and have that be the end of things."

Part of me felt like a lying fool. I could fix everything by confessing to Daddy . . . but the Law seemed to know about the Pritchards heading back to town, and if my plan to find their hideout actually worked, I wouldn't have to say a word and justice would still be served. Would one teeny-tiny night in jail be so bad for the Widow if it meant I could find proper evidence and get her freed the next day? Hard to say.

Miss Ada paused her pie cutting to pinch me. She angled her head toward Daddy.

"Ow," I murmured, rubbing my leg. "Yes, sir," I said to him.

"Good." Daddy scooted his chair back and stood up. "I'm going to check on your mama, then I'll be going back to the courthouse for a spell." He smiled at Miss Ada. "Mighty fine chicken, Miss Ada, thank you. Would you wrap up some of that pie for me to take along? I may not be home for supper, depending."

"That'll be fine, Judge. I'll leave a plate in the icebox."

Daddy left, and I sat stirring my gravy and green beans into a thick soup.

Miss Ada slid a slice of pie onto my plate and picked up Daddy's dishes and placemat. "All this fuss over a man with nothing to his name except some gold teeth."

"Who?"

"That dug up man. Heard some gossip at the store. Couple of women wondering why the Widow Douglas would dig up Amos Mutton when he didn't have anything to his name but the metal in his mouth."

"He had gold teeth?" I tried to picture a set of gold teeth and all I could see in my head were lumpy yellow nuggets. "I think I'd rather be toothless like the Pritchards. Say, Miss Ada, we got any cookies?"

She squinted her eyes. "Yes, Miss Becky. We got cookies, but I don't want you running off and using them as catfish bait, or whatever you have planned, you hear?" She disappeared into the kitchen.

"I hear," I agreed, following her with my plate.

She tilted her head at the jar on the counter. "Fresh batch from this morning. Now, I got some knitting to do, so you just stay out of trouble."

The cookie jar used to be my favorite thing in the kitchen, and not just because of what tended to be inside. Mama had painted it herself and let me choose the design. I picked daisies. She even let me help with one of the flowers, which is why one looked a little wild and ragged.

I traced the sloppy flower with a finger. "Yes, ma'am. I'll be good." I felt awful bad lying to Miss Ada, but I did it just the same.

There were about three hours before the sun went down and I had a handful of things needing to get done. Once Miss Ada went back into her cabin, I grabbed a dozen molasses cookies from the clay jar, sticking one in my mouth. I found an empty cornmeal sack in the pantry and crept over to the dining room cabinet for a couple of good linen napkins. We never had company anymore, so I knew the cloth wouldn't be missed. Rolling the cookies up tight in two napkins, I stacked them in the sack so they wouldn't break.

I added an empty oil lamp to the sack, a small bottle of oil, and a few matches. I wanted to change into Jon's clothes after I got to the cave, so I flew up the steps for a pair of his overalls and a shirt. Then it was back downstairs to borrow good paper and an ink pen from Daddy. I figured I'd run over to Amy's house and leave a note, on the off chance that plans didn't go as smoothly as I hoped. Tapping the pen, I sent a good splatter of ink across the paper and had to blow it dry before writing the letter.

Dear Amy,

I got an idea of where the Pritchards are keeping their

treasure stash. I'm not telling you
where because I don't want you
following just in case the outlaws
themselves end up being inside that
cave they mentioned back at the
cemetery. Whatever they stole from
Amos Mutton or his coffin will
surely be among their spoils, so the
Widow won't get blamed for being an
evil witch who digs up dead people.
Once I find the hideout for certain,
I'll leave a note for the sheriff
and he can set a trap and surprise
the Pritchards, like the Widow did
to Joe and Sid with her ghosty
sheets.

I might take Sid Sawyer with
me—only 'cause I don't care if he
twists an ankle or anything, not
because I don't love you the very
most! Plus, I know your daddy loves
you and needs you a whole lot and
it's got to be nice to be loved and
needed. You're my bosom friend and
I want you to have Jon's marbles
if I die (which I won't, I surely
promise).

-Your best friend, Becky Thatcher

Oh, and I got three good stinkbugs in an old tobacco tin under my bed. If I get caught by those Pritchards, please make an excuse to fetch the bugs from my room and put two in Tom Sawyer's desk (somewhere they're sure to get smashed) and one in Dob-head's black hair grease container. I got something of Ruth Bumpner's hid under there too, and I reckon you'll know what to do with it.

I waved the ink dry and folded the letter, trying hard to ignore the possibility that the Pritchards might've already gotten rid of whatever they took from Mr. Mutton. It didn't matter too much, anyway, I decided. The sheriff could still force a grave-robbing confession out of the outlaws without me being directly involved. And wasn't it the responsible and grown-up thing to do, letting the Law take credit for capturing dangerous criminals?

Why, yes, Becky Thatcher, I told myself. *Yes, it is.*

Nobody answered the door at the Lawrence house and I waited a good fifteen minutes before climbing a tree to get in Amy's bedroom window. I left the letter at the foot of her bed, hoping I'd be back with good news by the time she read it. An hour later, the day closing in on dusk, I was not pleased to see Tom on the Sawyers' front-porch swing. "Where's Sid?" I called from the steps.

"Out with Joe Harper."

"Where'd they go?"

"They wouldn't let on." Tom tugged on an ear and looked at me kinda shy. "You looking for someone to play with?"

I fixed him with a good scowl. "I *was* looking for someone to play pirates with, but not you, Tom Sawyer. You nearly got my hide tanned, didn't you?"

He blushed. "I must've been seeing things."

I stomped up the three stairs and poked his chest. "That's right, you were seeing things. Now stay outta my business. Why don't you go play with Sam Clemens. I reckon he's old enough for you to get along with."

Tom stared at his shoes, shuffling his feet. "His steamboat's all fixed up and he's leaving."

Well, shoot. I needed to see that man again about my marble sack and my promise to Jon. "When's he leaving?"

"Real early tomorrow," Tom replied. "He said around six o'clock in the morning."

Hmm. Daddy would either be busy or catching up on sleep tomorrow morning. Maybe I could sneak out and see Sam.

When I didn't leave right away, Tom Sawyer looked at me, a tiny piece of hope sparkling in his eyes. "Hey, if you want to, we could go find Sid and Joe. I overheard them saying they might go fishing and—"

"Just hush," I said, waving him toward the door. "I'm not going anywhere with you, Tom Sawyer." I turned and was nearly to the sidewalk when I began feeling a little bad about how I'd talked to him. Maybe he didn't understand what a pain he was. I spun around and leaned on the Sawyers' fence, facing Tom's cherry-colored cheeks.

"Sorry about that finger poke," I said. "Maybe you don't know not to tell on people. Listen, nobody likes someone getting them in trouble all the time and playing kissy-up to the teacher."

Tom's lip trembled, but he shrugged. "No one likes me anyway."

I nodded in agreement. "That's true enough. But maybe they would if you'd be more like a normal boy instead of trying to get in good with your aunt and Mr. Dobbins."

He breathed out a sigh that sounded way too grown-up for his ten years. "What's the point? Sid's never going to like me."

I was feeling generous for some reason, maybe because in the back of my mind I thought there was a slight chance I might run into the Pritchards and I wanted to leave life on a friendly note. "Tell you what. You want to earn Sid's respect?"

He nodded eagerly.

"You got to do something awful like pull down the laundry line, mess up the kitchen, or take out your aunt's stitching. And spit."

"Spit?"

"*Spit*, Tom Sawyer. You got to spit more if you want to get any respect."

He bobbed his head, as though committing my words to memory. Maybe there was hope for him after all.

"All right, then, I'll see you at school tomorrow."

"There's no school tomorrow," he said.

"What?"

"Mr. Dobbins has taken sick. He put out notice that there's no school this week. They announced it at Church."

I slapped the fence and gave Tom Sawyer a genuine smile. "Well, see there? That's the kind of information you should be spreading with those loose lips of yours. I like you better already."

He grinned and got even redder than before. I didn't like the look on his face. There was something too grateful about it. Closing the gate behind me, I set off to get better acquainted with the Widow's dog.

Charlie was waiting on the back porch. He plopped down on the steps as I got to the Widow's, just like he'd been expecting me.

"Charlemagne," I said, thinking it best to be formal when we were still getting to know each other. "Would you like to help me get your missus out of trouble?" I held out a cookie and watched the hound snatch it and wolf it down.

I swear that dog nodded while he licked my hand clean.

"Good boy. We'll be hunting down the loot from those men in the graveyard. The men who took Mrs. Douglas's shovel. You remember?"

He whined and licked his behind. I wasn't all too sure if that was a positive sign or not.

"Well, where's the scrap of shirt you ripped off that Pritchard?" My eyes drifted to his house. "Mind if I take a little look-see in there?" I tossed him another cookie and poked my head in. Sure enough, right near the back was a torn up piece of shirt that sure didn't look like it belonged to an old lady. There was also a familiar-looking sack. It was the dead kitten! Amy must've forgotten about it and Charlemagne had taken it in.

Feeling dirty just touching it, I used two fingertips to grasp the kitten bag and stuffed it into my cornmeal sack. I'd give it a proper burial later for bringing us luck with the Widow's bet. Then I went back for the cloth. It was stiff, probably from dried slobber.

"Now, Charlemagne," I said, "I suspect I know where the Pritchards might have hid everything they stole, but you'll be able to sniff those two out for certain. Besides, I wouldn't mind a little company. Here, smell it real good." I thrust the piece of shirt into Charlie's nose and he growled.

The growl sent tingles up my back, like someone was trying to play piano scales on my spine. I shook off the nerves. "That's right boy. We're gonna find the Pritchards' hideout and then we'll let the sheriff take over. Easy as pie. Are you with me? Get a good sniff on it now."

Holding my breath, I tucked the shirt piece into my overall bib and set off toward the woods behind the Widow's home. The dog trotted behind me for half a dozen yards, then held back.

I turned and saw that his ears were pricked up. I froze, looking around and seeing nothing. "Let's go, boy! Got to get this done while there's still a little light out. I have a mind of where you can find more of this scent and save your lady from jail. Sound good?"

The ears stayed up, like somebody had tied fishing line to them from the sky and was yanking away.

"Come *on!*" I patted my leg until it felt sore.

Finally, the dog moved, but instead of coming toward me, he loped around to the front of the house. My confidence dropping an inch or two, I turned around and headed into a patch of woods. Seemed I'd be doing my hideout hunting without Charlie's help.

I jumped the stream and hiked around the tree-covered side of Carver Hill, thinking maybe discovering the Pritchards' stash wasn't such a grown-up decision after all. My steps slowed while I pictured the graveyard scene from a week earlier. Shaking off the image of outlaws and knives, my black braid caught on a low-hanging branch. As I untangled it, I thought about how Jon had gotten Daddy's light locks and mine matched Mama's hair color perfectly.

I wondered if she'd ever brush my hair again. I wondered if, after the Widow was cleared of charges and the Pritchards were caught, I might try a little harder to talk to Mama. Maybe I could find a way to help her out of the dark place she was stuck in. My inner voice whispered a suggestion.

Maybe you should turn around and talk to her right now.

No sooner had I cleared the trees and stepped up to the school picnic grounds, feeling confused about whether or not to go home, than the Widow's dog came bounding up behind me. He near scared me to death and relieved me to pieces.

"You came!"

His mouth was full of weeds, which he dropped at my feet. He sat back, looking like he expected a reward.

I scratched his ears real good. "Well, I guess you didn't abandon me after all. What did you bring me?" I glanced at Charlemagne's offering, then bent for a closer look at the weather-dried plant scraps. They weren't weeds at all. I picked up a handful, ignoring the slobber, and stroked a faded white petal.

"Daisies?"

The truth dawned on me, like a glorious burst of day after a real long night. Or like two arms wrapping around me. Two Jon arms. I plopped down right in the meadow, astonished. "Charlemagne," I whispered. "Did Jon tell you to bring me these?"

He didn't respond, but he didn't have to.

I'd been so busy thinking about Mama that I forgot about my marble promise to take Jon on adventures. Maybe sneaking out to find the Pritchards' hideout was a *slightly* roundabout way to take responsibility and act grown-up, but it was a direct path to keeping my promise to Jon. And if keeping a promise wasn't the responsible thing to do, I couldn't figure on what was.

Mightily pleased at my intact sense of morality and ability to make smart decisions, I took a big inhale of air and let it out slow. "Okay," I said to the darkening sky, "let's go, Jon." I kissed the daisies, nasty and wilted as they were, then looped the group of them through Charlie's collar with shaking hands.

"You're a good boy, Charlie," I said, feeling fidgety but renewed in purpose. "The Widow said you gave messages from the Beyond and I guess she was right. Now, are you up for a little cave exploring?" I pulled out the cloth scrap and let him get another good sniff.

We were thirty feet from the cave entrance when that dog started going crazy. He jumped, barked, twirled, and sniffed. He wiggled like a worm, making his way straight inside.

The entrance cavern was about the size of the schoolhouse room and a good twelve feet high. With a small amount of light still hanging in the sky, the cave wasn't particularly spooky, but it went in quite far. Sid said that a young boy got lost in there years ago. Twenty feet back, the cave branched off in two directions. There was nothing on the rocky floor but a few blown-in leaves, a scattering of bird feathers, and a pile of dried poop. Looked to be fox droppings. More critter leavings were likely to be deeper inside the cave.

But there was something else. A smell like stale wood smoke and a feeling that somebody, or a couple of somebodies, had been where I was standing not too long ago.

Crouching behind a natural corner on one side, I stripped off my dress and pulled Jon's clothes out of my sack. *It's just the dried leaves,* I told myself, *reminding me of a burn pile, which makes me think of smoke.* I started to pull on Jon's shirt and overalls, when Charlemagne stopped sniffing and froze. Even his hair looked stiff. He turned and let out the most horrifying, threatening, wet-pants-causing growl I'd heard from him to date.

OhGodohGodohGodohGodohGod.

"Hey!" a voice shouted.

I whirled around, ready to face the Pritchards and my own death. When I saw the intruder's face, I collapsed into the corner, shaking in relief. "*Darn* you, Tom Sawyer! You scared the bejeezus outta me. And you could have seen me in my underthings!"

Tom looked horrified. "I didn't know you were taking your clothes off, honest! I just thought maybe we could be friends. I ran off, see? I didn't even tell Aunt Polly where I was going." He took a hesitant step toward a drooling Charlemagne, who seemed to realize that Tom Sawyer wasn't a danger to anybody but himself. "Is that Widow Douglas's dog?"

I fastened my overall straps and plucked Jon's marbles from the cornmeal sack, putting them in my front pocket for closeness. Then I stepped toward Tom, glaring.

He gave me a faltering grin. "What are you doing? Can . . . can I join you?"

Though I would've been grateful for nearly any human company, I was jumpy enough without having to worry about Tom Sawyer's safety. I'd also started to get a real creepy feeling about the cavern. Like maybe I was in the exact right spot, which was also the exact wrong spot.

If I was going to be making mistakes tonight, I didn't care for anyone to be affected by them except me. Jon and Charlemagne would be all the help I needed. Plus, if I died, Tom Sawyer had to stay good and alive to get those stinkbugs Amy would put in his school desk.

That decided, I gave him a big smile and ruffled Charlemagne's ears. "Join me? Not unless you want to go Pritchard-hunting with us. See?" I squatted down and stirred at the dried poop with a stick until it was good and broken up.

Tom stepped forward to see.

"Lookee there, it's Billy Pritchard's signature brand of tobacco." I pointed to the pieces of poop. "Some people would say that getting your hands on all that stolen loot isn't worth getting stabbed a time or two by the Pritchards." I swallowed a big lump in my throat, trying hard not to think about getting stabbed. I forced teasing and lightness into my voice, even though I was feeling fearful myself. "But I say, what's life without a little adventure? It might just turn out okay. You with me, *friend*?" Part of me prayed for Tom Sawyer to prove me wrong and still want to come.

But the blood drained from his face until he looked like a freckled ghost. Then Tom turned and ran off, just like I knew he would.

Slapping my legs for courage, I faced the rear of the cave and approached the two tunnels. The left tunnel was a dead end ten feet in. Backtracking, I took the right fork, feeling along the jagged walls to keep steady. Charlie walked a few paces ahead after a little prompting. There was a drip-drip-drip coming from somewhere deeper in the darkness. I filled the oil lamp from the bottle in my sack and lit its wick.

"Let's make this quick, Charlie."

But after a time, the walls got closer together and the ceiling started to slope downward. The cave smelled sickly sweet and mildewy, almost like body odor mixed with . . . I wasn't sure what. Charlie slowed down, finally stopping at another intersection.

"Come on, boy," I said, but Charlie wouldn't follow me any farther. He just growled and whined, gripping the back of my overalls with his teeth. He pulled at me, but I yanked free and gave him a little scolding.

"Now, stop that! You don't have to go down there, but I'm going."

The dog whimpered and went for my pant leg again.

"Go on," I said, shoving him. I pointed firmly back the way we came. "It's okay, boy. You just go wait by the entrance." I grabbed the wilted daisies from his collar and stuck them under Jon's shirt, right next to my pounding heart. *Keep me safe, brother.* "I'll be just fine."

Charlie let out a mournful howl.

"Shh! Now go! I said I'll be fine. I *promise.*"

But I shouldn't have promised. As I watched the tail end of my guard dog wiggle away, my mind connected the dots and realized what the sickly sweet smell was.

It was the same odor that had risen from Joe Harper's cigarette—the cigarette made from expensive tobacco that he found behind the school. Reed's brand tobacco. The same brand of tobacco that was stolen from the dry-goods store by thieves who were also fond of sweets.

I listened for noises and crept quietly ahead, certain of nothing except the fact that each step put me closer to the Pritchards' hideout.

Chapter Fifteen

Pritchards, a dead cat,
and a dead Pritchard

After just a few turns, a side tunnel led to a cavern the size of a rich man's parlor. The Pritchards must have been smoking cigarettes like crazy, because rolling papers and tobacco were all over the place. I picked up a tin and saw the Reed's label.

In the center of the cave was an ashy fire pit. A sofa-wide stack of boxes about four feet high was covered with a canvas tarp along the far wall, opposite the entrance. The stash. I hopped over the pit, set down my lantern, and commenced to checking out the loot.

Hooey! There were stacks of dollars, bags of coins, jewelry, cases of beer and whiskey, a bunch of men's belts with shiny silver buckles, and a whole box of Brinker's sour balls and taffy. *No wonder they've only got a few teeth left.* There was nothing that looked like it came from a dead man's grave. I'd have to settle for evidence of their general thieving, which I'd leave at the sheriff's office along with a note indicating that the Law could find more spoils at the cave.

I put a bound stack of dollars and a bag of coins into my sack. Those coins were packed so tight they didn't even jingle. I hefted my load and swayed it side to side, surprised to hear a muffled laugh. But the chuckle wasn't coming from the bag in my hands.

For a long second, my body turned into a hunk of rock and my head wouldn't even move to look in the direction of the noise. When it did, I nearly fainted because, Lordy be, if there wasn't a glow coming down the tunnel!

The voices heading toward me didn't sound like Charlemagne or Tom Sawyer, and the language was too coarse for any adult from St. Petersburg. My hands went numb, then prickly. Shaking, I set Miss Ada's cookies on a flat rock near the fire pit. I'd brought them just in case the Pritchards made an appearance and I needed to appeal to their rumored fondness for sweets. A pile of cookies was a weak trade for my life, but maybe eating would distract them long enough for me to slip past.

But maybe it wouldn't. I heard myself let out a strange, high-pitched chirp of fear. Swallowing hard, I tried to get the knot of dread down past my throat. With a desperate glance around the cave for a hiding spot, I sprang behind the booty and blew my lamp out.

All I could see was a thin circle of moonlight, shining in from a hole in the cave's ceiling. And all I could hear were the steps of the Pritchard brothers (who may have *killed* a man or five, depending on who you asked) coming my way.

They entered the hideout without noticing me, grumbling and passing gas and setting things down. I heard one of them digging around the fire pit. A low glow filled the cave with the soft bouncing light particular to wood flames. When I was certain they weren't going to add any freshly stolen goods to the pile I was hiding behind, I risked a peek. There was a nice little watching space between the cave wall and one side of the stack.

The taller one, Billy, was taking a long gulp from a bottle. His back was to me.

Forney had already discovered my stack of cookies and was pawing through them. "Lookee here, brother!" he crowed. "I got me some sweets." He ripped into one and his mouth turned upward in a bliss I knew well. "Good ones too."

"Will you *shut up*," Billy said. "You're too dang loud! And where'd you swipe them cookies from, anyway? I told you not to rob another store in this town. Leastaways not for candy and such."

"I didn't swipe nothing from this town but what we swiped together. These cookies were sitting right—"

Billy snatched the cookie from Forney's hand and threw it into the fire. "And you *know* that man told us not to eat so much sugar, 'specially not until these nuggets settle in. Don't you want more than one solid tooth?"

What man?

Forney's lips trembled. "Sure, Billy. But he had to rip the rotten ones out first, and that last one hurt awful bad."

Billy snorted. "If you think it was bad on your end, you

should've seen him trying to pull the goods off that dead man. The girl I caught spying on us was shaking less than him." He pressed one nostril and blew the contents of the other across the cave. "Gotta give him credit for finding us and coming up with the idea, but trusting a couple of outlaws? What an idiot. Any blame comes to us for digging up that body, he'll take it."

Hmm. So they had an accomplice in the cemetery. I'd seen Billy close up, but he must've brought someone other than Forney to do the dirty work. And I still didn't know what it was they stole from Amos Mutton.

Smoke started burning the bottom of Forney's shoes where his feet were too close to the fire. He winced at the smell a good minute before pulling his boots back. "You said yourself that man's an idiot, so I don't see why we should even listen to him, especially when he's saying I can't have a cookie."

Billy sat on the cave floor and tossed Forney the liquor bottle. "What kind of outlaw are you, whining about cookies? Jesus and Judas, *grow up!*"

I felt a little bad for Forney in that instance. People were always telling me the same thing. The feeling didn't last long, though, because when Billy turned toward the pile, he yawned. With his mouth open wide, I saw something glint in the firelight.

Whoever said those Pritchards didn't have any solid teeth was wrong. Billy Pritchard had two or three of his bottom teeth and two or three of his top, by the look of it. Gold teeth.

Gold teeth like Mr. Mutton who got dug up.

Gold teeth that looked just like shiny corn kernels.

Shiny corn kernels like the ones in Mr. Dobbins's locked drawer.

It clicked into place, piece by piece. Mr. Dobbins used to be a dentist. . . . He was about the same height as Forney and had the same longish hair. . . .

That was Billy and *Mr. Dobbins* in the graveyard—Dob-head was helping the Pritchards!

And his *ankle.* I bet Charlemagne had gotten Dobbins right on the leg before ripping a piece from Billy's shirt. Old Dob-head dug up that body and did his dentist work on the Pritchard brothers, putting in those gold teeth. That was the terrible moaning in the school that night. It was the sound of rotten teeth being torn out and Mr. Mutton's gold teeth being jammed into the Pritchards' mouths.

All the evidence needed to save the Widow Douglas was right behind the Pritchards' crooked lips.

A blast of hot breath hit me square in the neck. In my shock over the teeth, I didn't notice Forney moving around the back of the loot pile. Before I could scramble away, he'd yanked me by the back of Jon's overalls. I held on to my cornmeal sack as he pushed me into the light of the fire.

"Well, well, big brother, lookee what I found when I was going to take a pee."

Billy was bent over the fire. "How many times do I have to tell you, don't pee in here! Stinks up the whole—" He looked up and stopped talking, cocking his head to the side.

Forney shoved me forward. I stumbled to my knees and crouched there, fear making every inch of my body feel hot and icy at the same time.

Billy Pritchard reached for the long knife strapped to his

hip. Seeing that my eyes were glued to the blade, he pulled it out real slow, letting it catch the firelight. He stared at me and smiled, licking his lips. "Well, little brother. That is a fine treasure indeed. Do you want me to kill her, or should I let you have a murder to your name too?"

Thoughts whipped around my mind real fast, like a load of fireflies in a jar. The one I managed to grab onto was Miss Ada's voice from one of the many times she chided me for warming up to Jon's advice: *Your brother heard that nonsense from a fool, Becky. Superstitious folk go around believing anything, if you say it in the right voice.* Billy had been paranoid about getting his gold teeth put in under a full moon, so most likely he had other beliefs too. But how could I use that to my advantage?

"You'd better let me go!" I backed away from the fire, plastering myself against the stash and praying for an idea.

Forney laughed and reached over to me, his fingers closing again over my overall straps. "What for? So you can run out and tell on us?" Lifting me with a grunt, he jerked his arms over the fire and let me dangle there. "Not likely, Missy. You're headed for a bad place."

"I'm already in a bad place," I pointed out.

He looked at Billy. "She's right."

"Hell!" yelled Billy. "We're gonna send you to fire and brimstone!"

I managed to twist and kick Forney in the stomach. When he dropped me, I barely missed the flames. Before I could dash to the tunnel, the two brothers retreated to block the exit,

Forney on the right and Billy on the left. Both had knives out, the tips pointing right at my guts.

"Actually, sirs, you don't want to be hurting me," I said quickly. "You got gold teeth, don't you?"

Billy sneered, revealing a glint in the lamplight. "That's right."

"And I'm getting 'em next," said Forney. "Only got one in me before it hurt too bad. He had to pull out all our bad ones first and Billy took all the whiskey to suffer through his treatment. There warn't none left for me and—"

"Hush up!" I yelled. "Any fool knows gold teeth don't mix with cursed dead cats in the moonlight." I pointed to the stream of light coming through the ceiling.

"What dead cat?" Billy asked. "I don't see no dead cat."

I dug into my cornmeal sack. The kitten had decayed quite a bit in the last week and was a fearsome thing to behold. Stinky, too. I held up the carcass with my right hand, keeping the sack in my left. "This dead cat. Cursed it myself, the same night Mr. Dobbins dug up that body for its gold teeth! All I got to do is rub it on you and you're doomed."

I thrust it toward Forney and he staggered back.

"When this cat touches a man with stolen teeth," I hollered, "that man will drop dead! And if the stolen teeth are made of gold, that'll make your deaths all the more painful. Any fool knows that."

Billy eyeballed his brother. "Forney, grab her."

Forney, I was happy to see, was trembling so hard his knife shook. "I don't reckon I will, brother. You do it."

"Little brother," Billy growled. "Get over there and tie her up, or I'll stab you in your sleep tonight."

Lips twitching like he was trying not to cry, Forney started my way.

I nodded at him. "Come on then, though it's a shame your brother's using you to test the curse. All the same, I can't say I'll miss you much."

He gave Billy a wary look.

The older Pritchard's eyes went from me to the cat to his brother.

"Here," I told Forney. "I'll bring it to you." In a fit of nerve, I shot forward.

Forney's high-pitched squeal turned into an all-out scream when I reached up and rubbed the dead kitten in his face, pressing it into his neck and ears and mouth and dropping it down to his heart for a good rub there as well.

Before they could figure out my bluff, something curious happened. Forney's eyes nearly popped out of his head before they rolled back, leaving just the whites flickering in the firelight. He stumbled to the right side of the tunnel exit, reaching toward the cave wall for support.

And then Forney Pritchard dropped dead.

Billy stared at me, his mouth hanging open. His chest was going in and out real fast and his dirty fingers went in his mouth to touch his gold teeth. "He's . . . dead! You killed him! You and that dead cat killed my brother!"

I wasn't certain how to proceed. After all, I didn't know it was going to work. I hadn't even cursed the cat. Had Amy cursed it? No, that didn't seem likely. Anyway, I could tell Billy was half-terrified and half-rageful that I'd killed his brother. I needed him to stay on the side of terrified.

"There now, you see," I said, trying to control the wiggles in my voice. "I just wanted to be on my way, without any trouble. Now I guess I'll have to kill you, too."

Billy backed away from me, his body pressing against the cave wall.

I edged forward, dangling the kitten as a warning. "Now you and your gold teeth stay there." When I was two feet from the tunnel entrance, an awful thing happened.

Forney woke from the dead, moaning and rubbing his head.

Billy's face shot back and forth between the two of us, and I saw his rabbit-poop-size brain working. He sneered and raised his knife, jumping back in front of the exit.

"Why, you ain't killed Forney! He up and passed out or something!" Billy smiled at me, flashing yellow metal mixed with tobacco chew. "I think I'll kill you now."

Fear and regret froze me in place. Billy Pritchard's ugly face was the last thing I'd look upon, and all I could think about is how much I wanted to be safe at home with Daddy yelling at me for not acting more like a grown-up. Instead, I watched as Billy took his time stepping toward me, grinning his evil grin.

The truth will set you free, the Bible's John had said. I had the distinct feeling that I wouldn't be in such a mess if, up front, I had just told the truth about seeing the Pritchards in the cemetery. But I'd learned the lesson too late. The Pritchards would go free, the Widow would go to jail, and as for me, I was fairly certain that I was about to die.

No, a voice whispered. I couldn't tell if it was Jon or my conscience. *Becky Thatcher, you're going to fight for what you've got left,* the voice said.

In slow motion, my eye caught the edge of something white by my foot. One of the limp daisies had worked its way down my shirt and pant leg.

You still got living to do.

And that, right there in a cave with two murderous outlaws, was the moment I decided that maybe growing up wasn't such a bad thing. In fact, under the circumstances, I was desperate to give it a try.

I swung my evidence-holding sack in a circle, wondering how much damage a sack of coins could do against a knife. Trying to scramble away from Billy, I felt a hand grasp my ankle. Forney had recovered enough to yank me down to the cave floor where my forehead skin split open so I could hardly see from the dizzy pain and mess of blood.

Still holding the kitten by the tail, I whapped at the younger Pritchard a few times before he took sight of the whiskers and fainted again.

By then Billy was nearly upon me and I was out of curses. My heart hurt something awful. Knowing you're gonna die is one thing, but knowing that your death is going to be particularly painful is another.

My eyes burned, half from frightened tears and half from the fire's smoke.

Fire.

Throwing the kitten at Billy to buy time, I backed up to the fire pit and grasped the end of a glowing stick. With a deep and hopefully-not-final breath, I charged forward, prepared to plunge the fiery embers into Billy Pritchard's face, taking a slice from the knife if necessary to reach the tunnel.

"Stop!" came a shout from way down the tunnel.

Me and Billy both obeyed.

"Jon?" I called, convinced his spirit had been following me around the whole night.

"Who's Jon?" Billy turned to face the entrance to the tunnel, and that was enough for me. I dropped my sack, jumped over an unconscious Forney, and scooted past the distracted Pritchard brother. I ran straight down the tunnel, Billy swearing terrible things as he followed.

A rock tripped me and I flew forward with the fiery stick, feeling my knee scab break open in an explosion of pain. It made me light-headed, but the grip of a sweaty hand on my ankle brought me back. I kicked hard and felt his fingers slip off.

Scrambling up, I turned and flailed with the stick until I made contact with Billy. He yanked the ember side of the wood from me, screamed from the pain in his burning hand, and let it go. Hot blood trickled down my split forehead and leg scab, sticking to my hair and the inside of Jon's pants, but I kept moving forward.

Billy let out a holler as I rushed around the last tunnel curve and sprinted straight into . . .

Daddy? All six foot four of him was there, squeezed into the tunnel, wrapping his arms around me.

"Becky!"

"Go, Daddy! Billy Pritchard's got a knife!"

Daddy shoved me toward the exit and we both got to the entrance cavern about three seconds before Billy Pritchard came growling into view, cradling his hand and cursing.

I ran to the cave's opening and saw a crowd of people running up the hill, led by several charging hound dogs, including Charlemagne.

"*Run*, Becky," Daddy ordered.

"I'll murder that girl!" Billy snarled, daring to take a step toward me.

"Over my dead body, Billy Pritchard," Daddy bellowed. He was dressed in his judge robes even though it must have been about nine o'clock at night.

He held his arms wide, protecting me, and I swear that he let out a growl, though it might have come from Charlemagne. Either way, I'd never seen Daddy so fearsome. I must say, it was magnificent. My giddiness was halted by the wild look on Billy Pritchard's face.

"Your dead body? So be it, Judge." Billy laughed and advanced.

"Not so fast, Pritchard!" The sheriff had arrived, breathing heavy and wearing a badge that looked sweet as a bucket of ice cream to me. "Last time I checked, guns tended to be quicker than knives," he barked, pulling a pistol from his holster. Two deputies I didn't recognize had reached his side. They reached into hip holsters as well. Double hip holsters.

Five shiny guns pointed straight at Billy Pritchard. That was enough to send his knife clattering to the rocky cave floor.

I guess Billy didn't feel like dying that day, because he eventually let himself be tied up.

I let the Law know that Forney was unconscious and the sheriff sent the two deputies to fetch him. Five minutes later, they hauled him out. He was mumbling to himself and drooling a little. In fact, Forney Pritchard looked downright traumatized. He clutched the dead kitten.

"Quite the haul in there, Sheriff," one of the deputies said.

"Thank you, boys. Try to find an extra hard rock for the Pritchards to sit on and one of you keep watch while I finish up with Miss Thatcher."

The sheriff clapped a hand on my shoulder and handed me a damp handkerchief. "Looks like you've got some blood on your forehead, honey. Come on out into the moonlight."

I took the hanky and followed him to just outside the cave's entrance, dabbing the cloth against my forehead and picturing the scab that'd come of that cut.

"I'm sorry it took so long to get here," he said. "A sheriff downriver said the Pritchards were most likely headed this way, so we were already on high alert, but this grave-digging business took over. I was trying to depose Mrs. Douglas in court while several townsfolk looked on. It was quite the event. Seems there's not enough to do in this town, with those Bumpners pushing us to work on a Sunday evening. Tom Sawyer ran straight into the courtroom and wiggled like a fishing worm, but he didn't want to break up proceedings, I guess. Took him several minutes to open his mouth."

That Tom. Not even wanting to interrupt adults when my life was at risk. I guess I should've been pleased that he went at all. "I would've liked to have seen that," I said. "It was awful brave for him to have interrupted."

I reckoned I had to knock Tom off my enemy list, now that he'd saved my life with his tattling. I felt bad about tricking him with the poop, but felt even worse for having thought he was a chicken. Of course, he was a *little* bit of a chicken for not coming with me into the cave, but I don't blame him. That's the kind of chicken you feel downright grateful to.

"Certainly was, young lady. The Bumpners were high set on having an old-fashioned witch burning. Family of troublesome morons, those Bumpners. Tried to say Tom Sawyer was making up his story for attention. But not long after Tom told us where you were, a little girl named Amy Lawrence came running, waving a note that said you'd gone to find the Pritchards' hideout in the old cave. That was enough for me."

I got all prickly as the sheriff leaned down, wondering how I could have a bosom friend for over two weeks and not know she was a mind reader. How else could she have known I went to the cave? *Hmm*, I'd have to think on that. And while I sure was happy that the sheriff believed Amy over the Bumpners, it seemed I'd have to have a little talk with her about sharing personal notes with the Law.

"Listen to me," the sheriff said in a low voice. "I don't know how you girls were in a position to hear what a Pritchard said in the cemetery, but I'm inclined to just let that question fade away. It's embarrassing enough having a little girl know more about my town's goings-on than me." He winked. "I may have to recruit you as a deputy."

"Oh no, sir. I reckon I'm better at playing a pirate than a deputy. At least for now."

The sheriff laughed and eyed my forehead. "I'll need you to come in and talk with me tomorrow, sweetheart, but you should get on home unless there's anything else I need to know right now about what went on here."

I glanced back at the cave. The Pritchard brothers sat next to the rock where I'd changed into my overalls, appearing every bit the defeated outlaws. The dead kitten was still tucked into the crook of Forney's arm. He had something else in his hands too—a scrunched up bundle of cloth. "No, sir. I think everything else can probably wait for the sun to come up." *Wait, that's not true.* "Sir?"

"Yes."

"Except one thing."

"Oh?"

"You better go hunt down Mr. Dobbins and arrest him. He's been working with the Pritchards. He helped dig up Amos Mutton and yanked out his gold teeth, then he put the teeth into the Pritchards. It was him and Billy that night in the cemetery, so you can leave the wit—the Widow Douglas alone."

The sheriff snorted. "That's a mighty tall tale."

"It's true." Peering at the Pritchards again, I realized that Forney was wiping his panicked tears and snot on my dress. Well, that was one fishskin down.

"Hey, Forney!" I shouted. "Give me a smile and maybe they'll let you go free!"

Forney lifted his head and gave a hesitant smile. His one tooth gleamed in the lantern light.

"Well, I'll be. That's a gold tooth!" The sheriff rubbed his eyes. "Law up north said you fellas ain't got no teeth at all. Mighty odd." He walked over to the outlaws for a closer look.

Billy head-butted his brother so hard that they both fell forward and couldn't get up, their arms being tied and all.

"Ow!"

"Shut up, you fool!"

"You're the fool! And a mean older brother, to boot!"

"You're the whining-est, idiot-est, *stupidest stupid fool I've ever known*!"

One of the deputies gave them both a kick and they settled down. Daddy joined the sheriff and they spoke in low tones while I sat outside the cave, looking at the moon and thinking how it seemed to glow bigger and brighter than I'd ever seen. Maybe it didn't give off warmth like the sun, but a girl could look at the moon good and long without going blind, which was nice. It made me feel watched over. "Thank you, Jon," I whispered, taking out my marble sack, letting its weight rest on my bent knees.

"Let's get going, honey."

Brushing cave dirt from my overalls, I looked up to see Daddy's outstretched hand.

"Just a second," I said, his strong fingers gripping my arm and pulling me up. "I left something in the cave."

Daddy insisted on coming back with me, despite having to squeeze through areas no six-foot-four man should ever try to squish into.

I lifted the cornmeal sack. "We can go now."

"You came back for that?" he asked, looking surprised.

"Miss Ada can return sacks at the store for a little credit on the next bag of cornmeal. Plus, it has some lucky charms in it." Quite a few charms, I reckoned, from the weight of those coins.

Daddy let out a big sigh, but he was smiling. "Well I guess it's worth keeping, seeing as you're still alive, thank God."

"So the Widow Douglas won't be arrested, right?"

Daddy looked at me funny. "I suppose not. I can't quite figure on how you would know that Mr. Dobbins was at the—"

"Oh, the Pritchards were blabbing about it," I interrupted.
"I'm glad the sheriff is gonna leave the Widow alone."

After a long glance, Daddy smiled at me. "Let's go home."

But before we'd even made it to the school picnic grounds,
a woman carrying a lantern came running across the meadow
in a nightdress, calling my name in a panic. When she saw me,
she sank to her knees in the grass and began to cry.

I approached the woman and righted the oil lantern, touching the shadow cast by her shaking body. Shadows and footsteps and whispers. That's what she'd been to me for the last
year, and I wasn't quite sure how to handle having my mama
right in front of me. I moved her hands away from her eyes.
My own shadow darkened her features, but I saw her pain clear
as day. And it was for me this time.

"Don't cry, Mama." I knelt down and held her hands. I
hadn't held Mama's hands in a long time. I'd forgotten how
good it felt. She squeezed back, letting me know that she was
holding mine, too. "I guess maybe you still love me, after all."

Mama dropped my hands and wiped her eyes, sniffle-
snuffling. Then she lifted a set of trembling arms. They just
hung in the air, like she'd forgotten how to hug me. That
hurt my feelings a little and I felt myself back away. It was only
when a tiny cry escaped the back of her throat that I realized
something. She hadn't forgotten. She was afraid—not of hugging me, but of me not letting her.

The fear in her eyes settled all my resentment for good.

I leaned into her and pulled her arms around me. Hesitantly, then with more confidence, she held me in a tight, tight embrace—the kind that feels like the safest place in the world.

"Of *course*, I love you," she whispered, stroking my hair. "Don't you know that?" She pushed me away from her, searching my face for an answer.

I couldn't talk for what seemed like ages. What did I want to say, now that she was listening?

"Don't you, Becky?"

My voice felt unsteady inside me, even before I spoke. All the night's buzziness had worn off, and I was left feeling tired and scared and wanting my mama. I wanted her so much that I wasn't sure if I should answer her question. Part of me was afraid that truthful words might drive her right back into the darkness of Jon's death. The other part of me wanted more than anything to tell her how I felt.

When I did speak, it came out as a whisper. "I thought you were so busy thinking about Jon being gone . . . that you'd forgotten I was still here."

Her features wrinkled into a tight ball, twitching and twisting while she searched for something to say. After a moment, Mama's face smoothed into the sad expression I was used to. But it was different somehow.

I clung to that difference.

"Oh, Becky," she murmured. "*I'm sorry.*"

Instead of telling her it was okay, I started to cry. While Daddy came up and put his arms around us both, I cried in gratitude for my own life, which could have ended that very night.

While my family came back together, I cried in bittersweet

thanks for my brother up in Heaven, who I knew for certain would always be watching over me.

Most of all, while she tried her best to tuck me back into her heart, I cried in relief for Mama, who hadn't let me go.

Who was holding on to me.

Who still loved me after all.

Chapter Sixteen

---◆---

Saying good-bye

When I arrived at the steamboat at five forty-five on Monday morning, there were five men loading crates onboard.

"Excuse me," I said to a man crossing the gangplank to shore. "Do you know where I can find Sam Clemens, the boat pilot?"

The man pointed to the far end of the steamboat and I found Sam sitting on a chair next to a makeshift barrel table, checking a watch. His chair was tilted back to near-falling and his feet were on the railing, keeping balance. If I didn't have something else on my mind, I would've asked him how he managed it.

"Why, hello there, Miss Thatcher. That's a pretty dress, though I'd say the overalls suit you better." He tipped his hat.

Nervousness crept into my cheeks, but I set my mind to

the business at hand. "Sir, I need a favor. I made a promise to my brother—the one who died last year. Can you tell me if you're going to the ocean in this boat? I thought maybe you'd be heading that way, once the engine got fixed."

"This boat?" Looking up and down the length of the steamboat, Sam chuckled, "Not this one, no. This boat doesn't quite have the grit for that journey. It'll be headed back to Chicago."

I spotted a few fishing boats downriver. "Well, maybe some of them are?"

"Nothing that size is going down to the ocean." Sam fiddled with his pocket, coming up with a box of matches and his pipe.

I watched as one of the fisherman swatted at a bird picking something, probably fish guts, off his deck. "Sid said that he saw a raft last month, no bigger than something he and Joe Harper could put together. Two boys about our age were on it with a colored man. They were hooting and hollering about something, and Sid shouted over to see what the joke was. They were heading down to Louisiana."

Sam raised a thick eyebrow. "I hate to say it, but a raft with two white boys and a colored man is gonna have a hard time making it to the ocean without answering questions from people."

I dropped to the floor and pulled my knees up, hugging them. *What now?*

"Why do you want to get to the ocean so badly?"

I looked up at Sam and lifted my marbles. "To have adventures. I owe someone a promise."

He nodded, as though promises and bags of marbles went hand in hand.

"In that case, I happen to be taking over a ship that *is* going to the ocean. At least I aim to. I might go all the way across the ocean too, if I can get to the right starting point. As a passenger, that is, not as a pilot."

"You're not gonna be a river pilot any longer?"

"Oh, we'll see. Life has a way of messing with you if you make too many plans, but I'm hoping to be a serious writer one of these days." He pulled a small notebook and stubby pencil out of his pocket and waved them at me. "And not just for my own entertainment, either. Now, tell me about this promise."

"I just . . . I told Jon I'd take these marbles on adventures and he said that if he hadn't gotten sick, he would've gone to the ocean. He would've gone everywhere." I held the bag up and paused. There was too much snot in my nose and water building in my eyes to keep talking. This weepy crying business had to stop. Setting the marbles down, I took a hanky from my pocket and blew hard. I could feel a load of whiny tears pushing to get out and my throat felt like it had five cherry pits stuck inside.

Sam picked the bag up, politely ignoring my nose blowing. "What's so special about these marbles? I mean, other than the obvious fact that they're so special." He winked.

Tucking the hanky into my dress pocket, I stared at him real hard so he'd believe me. "A spirit man put a spell on those marbles and said that they'd carry a piece of Jon's soul always. It was Jon's idea."

"Sounds like a devil's deal."

"No, sir. There was no devil about the man, just a heapful of solid superstition. Said he could talk to folks after they stopped living and had gotten all sorts of tips from the Other Side. Anyway, I made a promise to Jon that I would make sure those marbles went far and wide."

Sam fingered the leather bag's ties and looked at me for permission.

I nodded and he opened it. He took out a bright green one, engraved with a delicate frog. He smiled real big and his fingers shook a little as he held it high. "Henry loved shooting marbles when we were boys."

"That was your brother who died on the river?"

Sam's eyes got misty. "That's right." He jammed a thumb in one eye at a time and rubbed. Taking a handkerchief from his shirt pocket, he blew his nose with a ferocity that rivaled Mama's worst snoring.

Remembering Daddy's words about mothers needing the most time to let go, I wondered how much time other people were expected to take when a loved one died. "Can I ask you a question, sir?"

He cleared his throat. "Certainly."

"Did people tell you to let your brother go and move on? I mean, is that part of growing up and all? My daddy wants me to grow up, and I'm . . . well, I'm determined to try."

He seemed surprised at the question and took his time thinking on it. "There were people who told me to let go of my brother, but I never paid them much mind. Souls that were connected don't get severed upon death. You bring along the best part of that person and you keep it with you always."

That sounded exactly right to me.

"Don't you worry, Becky Thatcher. Growing up has got

nothing to do with how to let a person go or keep them around."
With a nod at my dress, he chuckled. "And it has nothing to do
with whether you'd rather wear overalls or dresses."

Well, thank the Lord for that. I grinned. "Or whether you like
to spit cherry pits?"

"Well," he said, "that might depend on whose yard you're
spitting into. I'd steer clear of Aunt Polly's fence if you want to
keep your daddy happy." He raised an eyebrow and rolled the
frog marble between his palms.

Hmph. Didn't think he'd seen that. "That jumping frog was
one of Jon's favorites," I told Sam. "He loved frogs and toads.
He even tried to train one once, so he could make it hop higher
and faster than any frog alive." I felt my lips tug up toward
Heaven, remembering Jon in the backyard, baiting that frog
with dead flies, trying to get it to jump chin high. "Figured he
could use that frog in bets to win money."

"Isn't that a fine idea." Sam smiled and examined a few more
marbles—striped ones, ones with symbols, a couple made to
look like swirling storms—before putting them all back in the
sack. "You want your brother to get all the way to the ocean?
You want him to have adventures?"

I nodded.

Sam's eyes became twinkly. "I'll tell you what, Miss Becky.
If you tell me about your brother, I'll do my best to write him
into a story. And maybe if it's good enough, that story will
travel all over the world, so Jon will too."

"Put him in a book? You could do that?"

"There's enough characters in this town alone to fill a book.
And that Tom Sawyer has told me a thing or two."

I fought a sudden urge to spit. "I'll bet he has."

"You don't like him?"

"I've claimed him as a friend, I guess. Truth be told, I feel a little sorry for him. He's too scared to have adventures. A boy deserves to have adventures, doesn't he? Even if girls aren't supposed to."

Sam smiled at me, handed back the bag of marbles, and took a long pull on his pipe. He leaned in close. "Every man, woman, boy, and girl deserves to have a few exciting things happen along their path in life, Becky. Even if he has to make them up and put them into stories instead of living them. You just wait. The name of Tom Sawyer might have some adventures in it yet."

Well, I didn't rightly know what to make of that. "I don't know about Tom, but Mama and Daddy wouldn't be too happy about Jon being in a book without their permission," I warned him.

"I'll make it subtle. His name won't even be Jon. I doubt anyone would recognize him or you either, if I happened to put you in."

"Don't do that! I don't want to be in a book. I got plenty of time for my own adventures."

"All right, just your brother then."

"You promise?"

He raised his right hand and put the other one on his chest. "I swear not to undermine my own authority in matters of creating or not creating a fictional personality for you, Miss Becky Thatcher. I may have to slip you in somewhere, but trust me, nobody'll see a character named Becky Thatcher and ever think to associate it with the likes of you."

Hmm. There was something tricky about that, but I couldn't rightly make out what. "Well . . . good."

"I might even put a little romance into the book."

I thought of Mama's books and Sid Sawyer drawing pictures for Rose Hobart on his chalkboard and that dumb poem Pinchy-face wrote to Joe Harper. "Don't you go writing a romance book. Anything but that." I wrinkled my nose. "Nothing gets in the way of adventure like mushy love, sir."

"Every book needs a little love in it. And you don't need to call me 'sir.'"

"Should I call you Mr. Clemens?"

He looked far down the river. "Well, how about you call me . . . Mark Twain. I like that. That's what you call out when the water is deep enough to travel on. It's where a steamboat can float free on the river and won't get grounded."

It seemed odd, making up a name for himself when he already had one, but I didn't argue. "Mr. Twain, you got yourself a sack a marbles."

"You keep the sack. I'll take just one." He thrust his hand out.

I dropped the bag into it, wondering which he'd pick.

He sifted through them all, lifting and throwing them back. Finally, his eyes lit up. He squeezed the green frog marble between his thumb and forefinger. "Making bets on a jumping frog." He smiled. "I'd like to make sure I remember that." He dropped it in his front pocket. "Now, tell me about your brother."

What was the best way to start, when it came to Jon? "Well, he used to call me Daisy."

"And what did you call him?"

"I called him Huckleberry, on account of this one time he stained his hands so bad they stayed that way a whole week." I felt myself relax and grin. "They called him wild, and *he was*. Got up to mischief, but he had a real good heart. He had the wildest, free-est heart in the world."

"Huckleberry?"

"Huckleberry."

He wrote the word down.

Then Mr. Mark Twain and me sat and talked until the sun was fully risen. Until the steamboat let out three big bursts, indicating it was time for both of us to be moving on with our lives and heading forward.

Chapter Seventeen

———◆———

Resolution on Pinchy-faced toads
and Dob-heads

The next week was an all-out dust storm of lawful activity. It turned out that we would have more than just one week off from school. Mr. Dobbins got hauled into the jail and pleaded guilty the minute the sheriff threatened to put him in with the Pritchards. Word was, he squealed like a piggy when they pushed him inside a cell, saying he didn't mean to be an outlaw, he just needed enough money to start over as a dentist in a new town. He claimed that teaching little snots day in and day out had driven him batty enough to get involved with the Pritchards. He was going with the batty defense, which Daddy was not partial to forgiving.

The arrest called attention to the town and triggered a round of complaints from up and down the river. Apparently Mr. Dobbins had been traveling to do a little dentistry on the weekends. His tooth techniques were about as good as his teaching ones, it seemed.

The Widow Douglas, of course, was cleared on the charge of grave robbing and apologized to by the sheriff. Even after she was proved innocent, the Bumpners were so mad by the lack of town support in their campaign against her (not to mention the lack of an available teacher for their precious Pinchy-face) that they decided to move.

When Daddy told me that, I didn't even ask where the Bumpners were headed. I was too busy whooping my way over to Amy's house to share the good news. Having swiped Ruth's secret journal from the Bumpners' shed, I needed help deciding whether or not to give it back as a good-riddance gift. If I did return it, then I'd also need help gathering enough stink-bugs to put between the pages.

When I got to the Lawrence place, Amy was writing a letter to her daddy. She said that my letter had inspired her to tell him she didn't mind cleaning the house and getting meals ready, but she'd be needing a daddy whenever he could get around to it. She didn't know where to stick that letter and I suggested nailing it to the privy door because everyone goes there before long and that's where Mr. Dobbins always read the newspaper so it must be an all right place to read.

All the stolen loot got returned, and at church the following Sunday, Mrs. Sprague hugged me and Preacher Sprague called me a good and brave Christian in front of everyone, including Mama and Daddy. It was the first time Mama'd ventured into town and church since our arrival. I knew she was nervous, so I grabbed onto her hand, mostly to be nice, but also to make sure she would stay put. Mama's face was fixed with an expression that was more anxious than grateful, but she got a soft smile on her face when Preacher Sprague said my name during the sermon.

Daddy's big hand squeezed my shoulder and he whispered, "I'm awfully proud to see you growing up." Then he squeezed harder. "That said, I found the can of red paint in the shed. You're grounded for two weeks for painting those shovels and disturbing a legal investigation."

"But it was for a good cause," I whispered back, waving at the Widow Douglas, who had decided to get out of her house more often. Amy and I had gone back to visit with her twice since the stealing night and it was nice to see her taking my advice on how it'd be good to let people know that she was a friendly kind of witch.

"That's why I didn't give you a full month," Daddy answered, dropping a kiss on my head.

That same day in Church, the sheriff handed over the reward for catching the Pritchards, and with Amy's blessing, I gladly split it with Tom Sawyer. It amounted to a couple hundred dollars each, which I had to put straight into the bank. Mama said it would partly go toward decent clothing for me.

She planned on making my dresses herself, now that she was back to being a mama. Lots of dresses, she said, since most of mine were getting short in the ankle. A body can guess how I felt about "lots of dresses," but I swore I'd wear anything she made me, as long as I could keep Jon's clothes for special outings.

After the Sunday service, I told her how important it was

for me to keep talking about Jon now and then, and how it made me feel close to him to go gallivanting around the woods in his overalls.

She hugged me and said all right, as long as Amy was always with me and as long as I left a note telling where we'd be adventuring. We had ourselves an agreement, and a good one at that. Daddy warned me that Mama wasn't going to change overnight and that she'd still have a good amount of bad days, but that didn't bother me. I didn't mind waiting.

Miss Ada must have reckoned that I was fine and on my way to being grown, because she left for Chicago two weeks later. She and a friend of hers decided to open a blanket and clothing shop up there, and they'd both saved up enough money to make it happen.

The last thing she told me was to keep Jon in my heart. "He visits you all the time, you just don't know it," she said, fidgeting with her suit jacket. "Your brother's not here, but he's not gone either."

"I know he's not, Miss Ada." I pictured the daisies dangling from Charlemagne's mouth.

"Well, you make sure your mama knows that too." She smoothed my hair and sighed.

"I will, Miss Ada." I kissed her good-bye, feeling a selfish kind of sad that she no longer smelled like hotcakes, only like soap.

"I got to go," she said, digging at some dust in her eye. She touched my head again, her hand drifting down to cradle the side of my face before she left my life to catch up with her own.

I didn't even remember that stack of dollars and load of quarters until I dug the cornmeal sack out of my closet the same evening Miss Ada left. Wish I could say that the Good Lord prevailed upon me to turn it in, but the Good Lord was too busy with other business. Then I figured maybe that was God's way of saying I'd done good, so I kept it. A whole bag of quarters comes in awful handy when you like to make bets and you got extra time because your town can't find a replacement for the schoolteacher. As for that wad of dollar bills, I had plans for it.

I figured Amy and me would slip out early the next Saturday.

I figured we'd have ourselves an adventure.

I figured Mama wouldn't worry too much if I left the right note.

There was plenty of time to figure out the details. Life wasn't moving *that* fast. And just because I'd decided back in the cave that the journey of growing up wouldn't be so bad, that didn't mean I couldn't keep some things from my childhood and from Jon, just like Mark Twain said.

And if I chose to keep a little mischief, that was my business.

AUTHOR'S NOTE

The Actual & Truthful Adventures of Becky Thatcher takes place in September/October of 1860, a time when the real twenty-four-year-old Samuel Clemens—better known by his pen name, Mark Twain—was actively working as a river pilot on the Mississippi.

This novel is meant to be an origin story, suggesting that Clemens's *The Adventures of Tom Sawyer* (1876) was actually inspired by a happenstance stop in a small Missouri town during the author's river piloting days and, more specifically, by the adventures of a young girl he encountered there. The final scene with my Samuel Clemens character implies that, years later, he will write his most well-known characters (Tom Sawyer and Huckleberry Finn) as a disguised tribute to that same bold girl and her beloved deceased brother.

If you've read *The Adventures of Tom Sawyer*, you may have noticed that Mark Twain's Becky Thatcher character is a good deal different than the version I created. Like Becky, some of my other characters also exist in the original story in name, but their personalities and/or roles have been altered for my own purposes. The Widow Douglas is described in Mark Twain's book as pious and generous; in my novel, she is a recluse labeled as the town witch. Twain's Amy Lawrence was a past "love" of Tom Sawyer who makes Becky Thatcher jealous; in my novel, she is Becky's best friend. And the depiction of my Tom Sawyer as a friendless tattletale allows for the possibility that Mark Twain deliberately named his famous novel's lead character in order to give a lonely boy adventures as thrilling as the ones experienced by my audacious, mischievous, and morally-conflicted version of Becky Thatcher.

While certain aspects of my Samuel Clemens character are factual (Clemens did enjoy a good pipe and he did have a brother named Henry who died of injuries from a steamboat explosion in 1858), his personality, mannerisms, and dialogue in this novel are purely the product of my imagination.

Did my version of events really happen? Was Samuel Clemens truly inspired to write *The Adventures of Tom Sawyer* because of interactions with an intrepid young female? Well, no. (And another confession: only one of the "spells" Becky mentions in my novel actually works.) But I have no problem imagining that there were plenty of girls like my version of Becky during the 1860s. Girls who longed to break free of their dresses. Girls who liked to spit cherry pits. Girls who ached for the adventure and spirit that was often expected of and delegated to boys.

If you want to know more about who the *real* Tom Sawyer was based on, you might start by reading Mark Twain's preface to *The Adventures of Tom Sawyer*. And while you're there reading the preface, go ahead and read the entire book if you've never done so. It's a mighty fine story, as is its sequel, *The Adventures of Huckleberry Finn* (1884). I'd mention more of Mr. Twain's fine stories for you to read, but I've got a sack of cherries sitting on my front porch and a daughter who's ready to have her first pit-spitting lesson. And besides, I've got a feeling that you readers may have some mischief to attend to.

Happy Adventuring,
Jessica Lawson

The Actual & Truthful Adventures of Becky Thatcher

BY JESSICA LAWSON

Meet the irrepressible Becky Thatcher. She's a small-town girl in 1860 Missouri who loves a good adventure, especially if it means sneaking out of the house at night. Scary things like witches and dead cats don't bother her. She's ready for any danger, although witnessing a crime in a cemetery at midnight leads to even more trouble than Becky expects. You may have met a prim and proper Becky Thatcher in *The Adventures of Tom Sawyer*, but this one is much more fun and a great storyteller to boot.

PRE-DISCUSSION QUESTIONS

How is storytelling like lying? What kind of narrative and plot create an exciting story?

DISCUSSION QUESTIONS

SETTING

1. This story has a strong sense of time and place. Give details from the book about St. Petersburg and the different parts of it

that Becky frequents. What makes it similar to, and different from, where you live?

2. Describe Becky's house and what life is like there, including meals. What does Miss Ada do and how does Becky interact with her? What does Becky's mother do at home? How about her father?

CHARACTERS

3. Describe Becky's friendship with Amy Lawrence. Why do they become friends? How are they similar to each other and how are they different? What do they do together? How does their friendship change during the story?

4. Compare Sid and Tom Sawyer. What do they have in common? Describe ways in which they are different. Do either of them change during the book? How? Which of the two do you like best and why?

5. Describe Becky's relationship with Sid. Give examples of what they do together. How does she feel about him, and does that change? How does Becky feel about Tom, and why? Does their relationship change during the book?

6. Describe Sam Clemens, what he does, and what he's like. How are he and Becky alike? Why do you think the author included him as a character?

7. What does Becky believe about Widow Douglas early on?

How do her beliefs change, and why? Describe what Widow Douglas is really like, drawing from evidence in the story. What's her relationship with Sam Clemens?

PLOT

8. Summarize the opening scene of the book. What does it tell you about Becky's character and her situation? Use details to explain what this scene foreshadows about the rest of the book.

9. How does the bet about stealing from Widow Douglas propel the plot? What problems and actions does it lead to? Describe how the bet gets resolved.

10. Becky and her peers share a lot of superstitions. Describe some of them. What role do the superstitions play in moving the plot along? What purpose do the superstitions serve in characters' lives? Do any of the superstitions seem to be true beliefs? Are some of them false? Explain your reasoning.

THEMES

11. Everyone in Becky's household is grieving over the death of her brother, Jon. How does each of them—Becky, her mother, her father, and Miss Ada—deal with their grief? Give examples of how her mother's grief affects Becky.

12. Becky is a risk taker and often shows courage. Find examples of dangers that she is willing to face. How do her choices differ from what her parents want her to do?

13. Discuss the topic of truth and lying in this novel. In chapter 5, Becky explains her views on lying. Do you agree with her? Why or why not? She lies in chapters 9 and 14. Why does she do it? Do you think those lies are justified? Both Becky and Sam Clemens equate storytelling with lying. What do they mean? Why do you think the word truthful is in the book's title?

USE OF LANGUAGE
14. As a narrator, Becky loves a good simile. Make a list of similes that she uses and divide them into categories. For example, many of her expressions concern food, such as "different as cookies and collards," "red as a ripe apple," and "like cream on peaches." Do the categories fit well with the setting? What do the similes add to the story and the reader's enjoyment of it?

15. Take a close look at the chapter titles. What they foreshadow about the chapters they head?

The following discussion questions compare *The Actual & Truthful Adventures of Becky Thatcher* with *The Adventures of Tom Sawyer* and *The Adventures of Huckleberry Finn*.

DISCUSSION QUESTIONS
SETTING
1. The Mississippi River plays an important role in all three books. Discuss how that role is similar and different in the books. What does the river symbolize to the characters? How

do you think the author, Mark Twain, or the character Sam Clemens feels about the river?

2. All three books take place sometime in the mid-1800s. What are major differences between those times and the present in transportation, technology, social structure, and other broad areas of life? Give examples from the book. Find examples, too, of aspects of life in the books that are similar to life now.

CHARACTERS

3. Compare Becky Thatcher as a character in *The Adventures of Tom Sawyer* to what she's like in *The Actual & Truthful Adventures of Becky Thatcher*. Give details to describe similarities and differences. Why do you think Jessica Lawson changed Becky so much? Which version of Becky would you like as a friend, and why?

4. How is Becky in *The Actual & Truthful Adventures of Becky Thatcher* like Tom Sawyer in *The Adventures of Tom Sawyer*? Give specific characteristics and actions that are similar. What do they both like? What do they both dislike? In what ways does society treat them differently because of their gender?

5. Compare Becky's friendship with Amy to Tom's friendship with Huck Finn in *The Adventures of Tom Sawyer*. How are they the same? How are they different? What activities do both sets of friends share? How is Becky like Tom, and Amy like Huck? Use specific scenes and dialogue from the text in your discussion.

6. Give specific examples that compare how Tom and Sid act in *The Actual & Truthful Adventures of Becky Thatcher* to how they act in *The Adventures of Tom Sawyer*. Why do you think Jessica Lawson has made such significant changes from the Twain book?

7. What do you learn about Becky's brother, Jon, in the Lawson book? Describe some of her memories of him and the things she hears him saying in her head. Sam Clemens says he'll put Jon in a book, after which Becky tells him that her nickname for her brother was "Huckleberry." In what ways does Huck Finn in the two Twain books resemble Jon?

PLOT
8. Compare the plots of the three books. Give examples of how *The Actual & Truthful Adventures of Becky Thatcher* and *The Adventures of Tom Sawyer* are similar and different. In what ways is the plot of *The Adventures of Huckleberry Finn* more complex than the other two books?

9. Who are the villains in all three books and what do they do? How do they drive the plot? Compare them, discussing who seems most evil and why. Why did Lawson create new villains, even though she used many of Twain's other characters?

THEMES
10. Tom and Becky disobey a lot, and Huck breaks a lot of societal rules, but all three have their own code of ethics. Find

passages where each of them thinks about right and wrong. What does each one believe makes a good person? How do they try to follow those beliefs?

11. Near the end of *The Adventures of Tom Sawyer*, Tom is trying to convince Huck to return to the Widow's and be more conventional. "Everybody does it that way," Tom says, to which Huck replies, "I ain't everybody." Discuss specific ways that both Huck and Becky reject conventional behavior.

USE OF LANGUAGE

12. Huck Finn and Becky are first-person narrators. *The Adventures of Tom Sawyer* has a third-person narrator. Analyze the differences between the two types of narration, noting advantages and disadvantages of each in general and in these books. Describe the third-person narration in *The Adventures of Tom Sawyer*. Does the narrator ever address the reader directly? Review the definition of limited omniscient narrator and omniscient narrator, and discuss which type narrates *The Adventures of Tom Sawyer*.

13. Consider the amount of dialogue in the Lawson book to the Twain books. Evaluate generally how many pages in Lawson have no dialogue compared to the Twain books. Compare the length of paragraphs, too. Which style is most similar to books you usually read? Find some other children's books from the 1800s, such as *Treasure Island* and Louisa May Alcott's books. How do they compare to the Lawson and Twain books? Which style do you prefer, and why?

Get a sneak peek at Jessica Lawson's
new book, *Nooks & Crannies*!

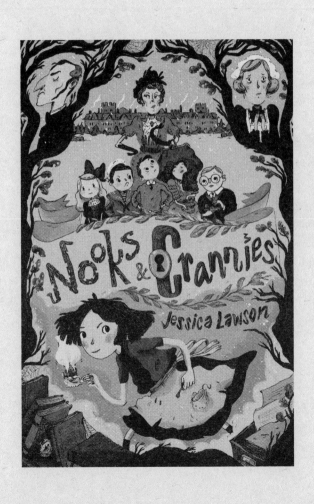

Just past three o'clock in the afternoon, when schools across London were releasing much-adored children by the bucketful, Tabitha Crum was ushered into the cold as well. She tarried at the edge of St. John's gate, threading an arm through the bars and observing the world for a moment, ignoring the jostling of boys and girls who seemed in such a hurry to return to the places they belonged. "Today," she whispered to a small lump in her satchel pocket, "we find ourselves in a curious situation, sir." Slipping an envelope from her bag, she lightly tapped it against the obtrusion. "Off we go."

The cobblestone streets in the village of Wiltingshire were made eerie and muted by thick November fog, and clip-clopping carriage horses snorted up and down the road, emerging and disappearing into the mist. *Almost like ghosts,* Tabitha mused. She clutched and rubbed the pretty envelope, letting one fingernail linger along the seam. The hand-delivery messenger had passed two letters to the teacher, glaring severely and emphasizing three times that they were *not* to be opened, but given to the parents of the children. What she and beastly Barnaby Trundle had done to deserve the elegant envelopes was unknown. The only certainty was that the glue was of a stubbornly good quality and Tabitha's nails were of a woefully short length.

"It's as though they've sealed it together with spite," Tabitha muttered to the pocket lump, earning an offended glance from a passing elderly lady. Whether it was the muttering, the remark itself, her outgrown uniform, her worn grayish schoolbag that resembled a mangy rabbit, or a combination, Tabitha couldn't be sure. Perhaps the woman was offended by children as a whole, rather like her mum and dad.

Licking chapped lips as she passed the corner bakery with its beckoning, sweet aromas, Tabitha felt a stirring in her belly unrelated to having eaten only broken crackers and cheese rind for lunch. Ludicrous or not, it was impossible to ignore the tiniest possibility that the envelope might contain . . . a small bit of light. Hands shaking from chill and an unfamiliar amount of prospect, she lifted the paper to her nose and took a long sniff. It smelled faintly of flowers.

A summons from Scotland Yard to become an Inspector-In-Training.

An invitation from King Edward to attend and gamble on a horse race.

Notification from a long-lost relative who actually wants me and wouldn't view me as an imposition.

"What's that, Pemberley?" Tabitha whispered to the lump, which was now squirming and fretting about.

Mouse whiskers poked out, followed by a mouse face. "I don't know how you manage to read my mind, but I suppose that's what best friends do. And yes, those are all unlikely scenarios, but it's nicer to imagine such things than to rip into the paper and find an advertisement for tooth powder or elocution lessons, isn't it?"

Not caring to dwell on the possibility of such disappointing contents, Tabitha was grateful when a distracting bellow sounded behind her. Oddly enough, the bellower seemed to be calling her name from the street. Before she could turn, a familiar bicyclist veered close to the curb and sprayed Tabitha with filthy water left by a midday storm.

"Your invitation is bound to be a mistake. There's no way she'll let you in!" yelled a horrid voice.

Wafting alongside the insult were the scents of burned toast and rotting cinnamon. There was only one boy at St. John's who wore such pungent odors. Sure enough, she turned to see Barnaby Trundle pedaling a slow circle in the road.

"Best to stay home, Drabby Tabby! I've heard the place is haunted and the spirits are hungry for filthy, ratty girls like you." Barnaby stuck his tongue out as far as it could go.

Tabitha wiped a muddy water streak from her face and flushed, both at the insult and the realization that he had opened his envelope and she had no idea what he was referring to. She thought of exactly seven things that she would like to do to her classmate, one involving a rather nasty collision with a refuse wagon.

Barnaby took one hand off the handlebars to send her a mocking wave before smoothing his reddish locks and disappearing around a corner.

Squeak!

Tabitha pulled Pemberley from the satchel pocket. "Nice and dry, are you? It was clever to tuck yourself away like that." She nodded seriously. "And yes, Pemberley, you're right. I should have defended us."

Squeak?

"Oh, I don't know, something like, 'Believe me, Barnaby Trundle, I won't be staying home. I rather think you should, though. I've heard most spirits have a fondness for repulsive boys with no manners and an excess of their father's hair crème. And an obscene amount of completely unnecessary aftershave. Any ghosts will smell *you* out in a minute.'" She let Pemberley sniff her hand for crumbs, run up her sleeve, and burrow under her shirt collar. "It's a shame I'm not just a bit bolder, isn't it? One day you and I shall make good on a bit of mischief."

Even soaked and unavenged as she was, a flutter of excitement warmed its way up Tabitha's back and neck, tickling the tips of her ears. *So, he's opened his.* And according to Barnaby, her envelope was a mistake. Based on the boy's despicable nature, his claim must mean that the contents were sure to be something quite good. *(Well done, Inspector Crum.)*

Tabitha put a pencil in her mouth as she walked along. Instead of reading through reports at the Scotland Yard office of the Metropolitan Police Service, Inspector Percival Pensive always did his deducing in a corner booth of his favorite pub, puffing a pipe or chewing pensively on his pocket watch chain. Neither pipe nor pocket watch was practical for an inspector of her youth and means, and so Tabitha made do with pencils. "Now, Pemberley," she whispered. "What could it be? Let's review the clues. Barnaby said to stay home, so that would make it an invitation to go somewhere. . . ."

Squeak.

"Yes, yes, a place owned by a woman . . . haunted, he said, though that bit was clearly rubbish." It would be easy enough to find out more. There was a moment, one brief moment, where the act of disobedience hung in the air like a buttered crumpet, waiting to be fetched and gobbled up. Tabitha's hand lifted the envelope, as though of its own accord, and her free fingers rose. Carefully, deliciously, she held her breath and began a tiny tear at the corner.

And stopped.

She sighed, dropping the hand holding the note to her side as she continued toward her home. *Tabitha Crum,* she scolded herself, *they'll never grow to love you if you can't even follow a clear and simple rule, especially one that was emphasized three times and accentuated with a glare.* A second voice, that of her mother, snuck in to repeat the answer to a much younger Tabitha's question. *You want us to love you, is that right? Love, Tabitha Crum, is to be earned, not given away to just anyone like a festering case of fleas.*

She'd been seven when her mother had made the comparison of love and irritable itching. Tabitha remembered the statement quite well because it was the same year children at school had suddenly gotten it in their heads that she had a case of head lice. That had been a different time and nobody had gotten close to Tabitha since. Of course, with the addition of a pet mouse over the last year, her lack of friendship could perhaps be further explained by the misapprehension that she spoke to herself. Pemberley was a most excellent consultant in all matters, but he tended to stay out of sight, so Tabitha could somewhat understand the slanderous comments.

Or it might have been the unfortunate, uneven, unattractive, blunt-scissored haircut her mother was so fond of giving her.

Or it could have been the simple truth that making friends can be an awkward and a difficult thing when it's a one-sided endeavor and you've a pet mouse and you've been painted as odd and quiet and shy, when really you're just a bit misunderstood.

In any case, nobody at St. John's seemed lacking for companionship except her. But Tabitha reminded herself that there were far worse things than not having friends. In fact, she often made a game of listing far worse things:

- eating the contents of a sneeze
- creatures crawling into her ear holes
- losing a body part (though that one was debatable, depending on the part. An ear or small toe might be worth a friend or two)

While Tabitha stopped to stare at fresh scones piled in the window of Puddles Tea & Confectionery and speculated whether the envelope's contents would outdo last year's Christmas box of used tights, two passing men knocked her to the ground, as though she wasn't worth moving for.

"Two more are floating around somewhere!" one of them said, stabbing a finger at his newspaper and not noticing her in the slightest. "It's simply *unfathomable*. After all this time? That place has got to be like heaven above! Gilded soaking tubs and secret rooms filled with money and the like. And to ask *children*, of all people. I say, Rupert, life is simply beyond unfair. . . ."

Tabitha picked herself up, slightly rattled. She sighed at the careless bumpers and at the memory of Barnaby Trundle's last words. Under normal, unsprayed circumstances she wasn't filthy, but she was skinny and knobby-kneed and wearing a uniform far too small for someone who'd grown several inches in the last six months. And apparently those elements combined to make her the sort of person who was prone to being callously clipped down without notice or apology.

"Oh, Pemberley," she said aloud, rounding the final corner before reaching her home and tugging on the end bits of her hair, wishing *it* would grow several inches, "if only life were like a book, and I could choose precisely what part I played." She ignored the puzzled glance from her neighbor, Mrs. Dullingham, who was leaning out of her door to fetch a grocery delivery. "If only the envelope contained a—"

And at precisely half past three, Tabitha stopped musing and walking, having spotted a curious sight outside her modest brown brick home: her father's briefcase, her parents' traveling trunks, and a jewelry case crowded together at the front entrance.

None of her things were among the pile.

When a wealthy recluse opens her home to a chosen few, secrets hide around every corner.

Mystery, murder, mayhem.
That's no excuse to be rude.

Jack Foster has stepped through a doorway into quite a different London.

"Full of verve and imagination. . . . The characters are ones you'll root for from the moment you meet them."
—Stefan Bachmann, author of *The Peculiar* and *The Whatnot*

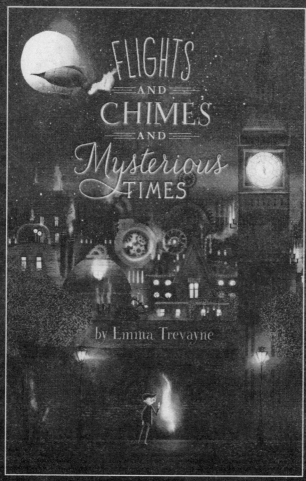

FLIGHTS AND CHIMES AND *Mysterious* TIMES

by Emma Trevayne